The Party Dress

KEVIN COYNE

SERPENT'S
TAIL

FIC.

Library of Congress Catalog Card No: 90–60286

British Library Cataloguing in Publication Data

Coyne, Kevin
    The party dress,
    I. Title II. Series
    823.914 [F]
    ISBN 1–85242–197–5

The right of Kevin Coyne to be identified as author of this work has been
asserted by him in accordance with the Copyright, Designs and Patents Act
1988

Copyright © 1990 by Kevin Coyne

This edition first published 1990 by
Serpent's Tail, 4 Blackstock Mews, London N4

Set in 10/13pt Bembo by AKM Associates Ltd, London
Printed on acid-free paper by
Nørhaven A/S, Viborg, Denmark

CONTENTS

Part 1

THE PARTY DRESS

It was untidy. It used to be the best room. There was a time when everything was in its place, when the four little lace table-mats were correctly positioned. This was a long time ago. Now the grandfather clock refused to work and the chair with the broken leg remained unrepaired. She was desperately old. Help was available but politely refused. Friends had given up on the problem. I was a child then.

I remember visiting with my mother. We always entered by the back door. The front one (never used) was thick with dirt and cobwebs. I thought this strange. When had it last been opened? Were we her only visitors? My mother sometimes made reference to another woman; a health-visitor who sometimes brought round groceries. I never met her, although I gathered (from the few times her name was mentioned) that she was regarded as an unwelcome do-gooder, a person to be barely tolerated.

It was a dirty house. 'Why do we have to come here?' I used to ask. 'Christian charity,' my mother would reply. I wasn't impressed. I didn't understand. What good did we do there? There were more important things to do.

The house was situated close to our parish church. It was on a hill overlooking rows of cramped red-brick houses and was quite large (certainly bigger than those at the foot of the hill) with a small garden at the front and a large one at the rear.

When the sun shone I played cowboys and indians, running hard over the neglected lawn, dodging in and out of the dead apple trees. If it rained I sat in the back kitchen, read comics, rummaged through cupboards. I was always glad when the time came to go home. I preferred my own garden, my own street, the company of my little friends. I made the best of a trying situation.

One rainy afternoon (I think it was in December) my mother summoned me into the old woman's living-room. 'Put that comic down,' she shouted, 'and come and help us out.' I was most unhappy. She knew I was afraid of that gloomy place with its smelly furniture and peeling walls. 'All right,' I called, putting a brave face on things.

The room was noticeably darker than usual. 'Who drew the curtains?' I asked nervously. There was no reply. My mother beckoned me over to where the old woman sat, small, shabbily dressed, mouth botched with lipstick. 'I want you to try this on,' she said, smiling and producing a pink and white party dress from behind her back. 'But it's for a girl!' I wailed. 'I can't do it.' 'I'll give you two shillings if you do,' said the old woman suddenly, eyes gleaming with excitement. I was persuaded; two shillings was a lot of money in those days.

It was a new and strange experience. 'How does it feel to be a little girl?' asked my mother, patting my backside gently. I wasn't sure. I thought I ought to be ashamed, but I wasn't. The old woman was delighted. 'They're so alike,' she said. 'Who?' I asked, curious. 'You and my little Linda who died,' came the tearful reply. After ten minutes I was asked to change back into my normal clothes. My mother took the two shillings (I protested, but was told it was 'For my piggy bank') and we departed.

The weather was turning to snow when we reached home. I was curious: why had we left so suddenly without the usual goodbyes? 'Will we be going again?' I asked. There was a pregnant silence, then she glared at me. 'You enjoyed wearing that dress, didn't you?' she yelled. 'You bloody well enjoyed it.' I felt my head sinking to my chest. I couldn't answer. She was right, in a way. 'Wait till I tell your father,' she continued, 'then you'll see what's what.'

I was suddenly very afraid.

MOMENTS

Today I walked across the silver green water and almost collided with a sailing boat. The trees surrounding the lake were rich with autumn colours; bushes with berries everywhere.

I had a deep wish to fly, but my temporary wings were damaged having been sat upon by a fat farmer from a nearby village. In a local café I observed men drinking and eating; their eyes induced feelings of sadness.

In my loneliness I developed an obsession for detail. I had a powerful desire to describe everything in a fussy Dickensian way in a language alien to my century. Nevertheless, despite the slight coldness of the morning, I resolved to keep a cheery smile on my face.

Two weeks later I was sitting at a window looking out on to a farmyard. The weather was good (if a trifle cold) and I was attempting to write a stylish novel. The fine weather had produced a renewed optimism – a sense of exultant release. I had little time for petty hatreds, water walking, or suburban megalomania: I was laughing.

Some days after the arrival of my new positive attitude I sensed the emergence of another depression: I fought it off. I gazed heavenward in the direction of some heavy Bavarian candelabra, and thought of Miss Haversham, of a dusty wedding cake, and ludicrous, lifeless senility. My girlfriend kissed me full on my bald spot, and I laughed like a happy child.

A dull Thursday found me wanting to write but unable to think of anything to write about. I chastised myself for my lack of imagination, producing an imaginary whip the size of a cobra. I dwelt in a mental cage. I cursed potty-training, mothers and all children at home. Someone presented me with a sticky bun: 'From Hawaii,' they said, 'with great love.' I felt special – like Elvis Presley.

Friday morning I woke up and *imagined* myself to be a goat (I stress the imagined, mainly because I'd been drinking heavily the night before). 'All a bit Kafka,' came the wifely comment from across the breakfast table. Sick at heart I walked to the river with the intention of committing suicide. On the way I met the ghost of William Blake. 'Nice day,' he called, as he rode by on his bicycle. I looked deeply into the heart of a nearby flowering shrub and changed my plans. 'Good old Bill,' said my wife afterwards, 'still keeping fit at his age.'

Three weeks afterwards I was meditating on my new found silliness, on my inclination towards the ridiculous. I'd never been sure of laughter before; now, I embraced it, pursued it relentlessly.

I need a God I thought, something serious to stop the giggling. That afternoon I met a Chinaman in the supermarket who, without any prompting from me, presented me with a copy of *Little Women* by Louisa M.Alcott. 'Why this?' I asked. 'Because I don't want it,' he replied. After I passed the check-out I noticed him giving a copy of *Fear of Flying* by Erica Jong to a balding pensioner. It was a funny day. When I got home my eldest son said he'd met a distant relation of Abraham Lincoln's who'd insisted he borrowed a battered copy of *Ben Hur* by Lew Wallace. We spent the night reading together.

The following morning I sat at my desk considering. I decided writing was essential for my brain, and that without it I would probably finish up a nutcase. And then, as is usually the case with me, I pondered on the benefits of physical exercise. From the top drawer of a nearby bureau I produced a letter from the Parent-Teachers' Association inviting me to participate in a charity football match. Two weeks previously I'd decided against taking part; now I felt differently. 'Why not?' I said as I went into the spare bedroom to look for my boots. 'Stanley Matthews played his last game at the age of fifty.' As I passed my son in the hallway I noticed he was carrying a copy of *My Psychic Life* by someone called Madame Ursula. I resolved to borrow it later.

The weekend (usually anticipated with excitement) was a disaster; a catalogue of madness and misconceptions. I fostered chaos, held its clammy little hand. 'Destroy everything,' said a voice (not dissimilar to my own). I tried to obey. I was precious, pompous, and eventually defeated by my own sick cleverness. I decided that one day I'd see a doctor, have my head examined. Sunday afternoon found me walking through a strange city, observing rather than participating, criticizing rather than helping. I felt my mad grandeur fade, my self-image reduced to that of a flickering flea – a speck of nameless dust. 'Fall back into line!' ordered the lusty sergeant-major. Leaning, as if in a dream, I touched his gleaming, senseless medals. Laughing, I put my head into his mouth.

One evening in early spring (I can't remember the exact date) my mind cleared; the savage fantasies disappeared. My wife made me a cup of herbal tea, presenting it to me with the immortal words: 'Feel better now?' Spluttering, as I sipped at the foul tasting liquid I answered in the affirmative. At this point the small white cat leapt from the arm of the settee on to my shoulder. 'A good omen,' she said. 'He seems to like you.' I was afraid it might mess on my clothes. I forced a smile, sweat running from my brow. 'Hot, dear?' asked my wife. 'Shit scared,' I replied. She looked at me, a puzzled expression on her face. 'Have you taken your tablets,' she whispered, a look of deep concern in her eyes.

The next day I woke up, a lively little story running through my head concerning a fireman, a budgerigar, and a Polish actress from Scarborough. As I lay half-asleep, my youngest son arrived at the bedside bearing a cup of coffee and two small pieces of toast, 'Diet day today,' he said, an impish smile playing across his face. I groaned, turned over on to my stomach, buried my face in the pillow. I wanted egg, bacon, tomatoes. 'Fucking diet,' I shouted, my anger muffled, but audible. 'Shut up!' came the sharp retort. Young Trevor was very quick tempered – he had little patience for a fat father prone to nervous breakdowns. Later, as I nibbled feverishly at the toast, I thought of another story: one about a duchess and a retired headmaster set in Middlesbrough during the war.

One Wednesday morning (long after my dieting days were over) I woke with stomach pains. After breakfast – large, greasy and definitely unpalatable to the more sensitive appetite – I took a brisk walk round the town. With surprise I noticed several of the larger stores were closing down. 'A sign of the times,' I said aloud, 'everything must change.'

The afternoon found me discussing Greek philosophy with my eldest son (something I know nothing about). He became insulting when I mentioned my religious beliefs. 'Typical ex-Catholic,' he groaned, 'can't get God out of your head.' That night I prayed for his soul; not out of any real conviction, more out of anger at his contempt. Late evening the stomach kept me awake, my loud farting upset my wife. 'Go to the spare room,' she said. 'You're so aggressive.' It wasn't the best of days.

Easter Monday I sat in a small bar listening to conversations. 'His head's so big,' said a fat woman to her friend. 'Yes,' came the whispered reply, 'and it seems to match his arse.' Tired of life's cruder element, I left the bar and made for a nearby church. On entering I passed a small person (it was hard to tell whether it was a woman or a man) cleaning the white marble steps. Everywhere was slippery with suds, quite dangerous in fact. 'Watch yourself,' warned the diminutive figure, 'you'll slip on your bum.' Inside the building I thought long about the merits and de-merits of the words 'arse' and 'bum'. My attempts at serious prayer were thwarted: I laughed out loud.

It was one week after Easter when – in a fit of abnormal sensitivity – I decided to move house. I was aware that, in many ways, it was a rash decision. However, one sunny afternoon, I took two books, six shirts, two pairs of trousers, three pairs of socks, five pairs of underpants and – without looking too far back – moved to Germany. The journey over was easy (although memories of England occasionally plagued my confused mind).

The first days in my new country were spent in imitation of Dylan Thomas: I drank too much. Later, after a view of a Bavarian forest by moonlight, I took to the imitation of Christ. I was close to a divine, mysterious madness, close to sprouting wings. I decided to mix truth with lies, speculate on the existence of heaven.

Almost one year later I was sitting in a small guest house near Frankfurt; I'd stopped drinking and was very irritable. 'Nice weather,' said the owner, his round face glowing with mock servitude, 'Yes,' I replied, 'and the lake's perfect for water walking.' His expression changed, disgust registered on his once friendly face. 'Was that a reference to Our Lord?' he asked, angrily. 'Are you taking the piss?' Shocked, I rose from my seat and made to leave. The owner barred my exit. 'Wait a minute,' he said. 'Aren't you Rocko Wilkins, the famous pop star?' 'Yes,' I replied, noting the fawning, adoring manner, the sudden change in attitude. 'What's it to you?' 'Well,' he said, 'I was just wondering. Was Elvis really a deputy sheriff? Did Jerry Lee

THE LAND OF SATIN DOLLS

It was a day of days, the day Henry's bed ascended through the ceiling. He was just a tiny bit surprised. It had been a busy week. 'Fuck it,' he bellowed as he ascended. 'This is great!' Lift-off was painless.

It was chilly out, a December evening just before snow. There were a few bedroom lights twinkling, the odd bus meandering towards the city depot. He pulled the counterpane up to his chin, looked up at the stars. 'Where to now?' he whispered. 'To the land of satin dolls,' called a voice in reply. He was taken aback. He didn't expect an answer. He closed his eyes, waited to arrive.

He woke with a start. 'Well I'll be blowed,' he said, taking in his surroundings. He was in a large blue bedroom, a soft yellow light created subtle shadows on the walls. He could hear the soft thud of bongoes, a woman's voice. After the initial shock he settled down to wait. Things were bound to happen.

Marion was the first to appear. She was small, blonde, with protruding front teeth; a girlfriend from boyhood. 'Hello, Henry,' she drooled, 'how's life down there?' Henry was astonished. 'Marion,' he whispered, 'I thought you died years ago.' 'I did,' she replied, 'but I'm alive again. This is the land of satin dolls, a place where the old-fashioned type of girl takes her heavenly rest.' Henry fell back on his pillow and sighed. 'Nice to see you,' he said, 'but you can go now. I remember you treated me pretty badly in the old days, left me for that pig Roger Twelvetrees.' Marion sat on the bed and started to cry. 'I came to say I'm sorry,' she sobbed. 'All right, all right, all right,' stammered Henry. 'You're forgiven.' Marion stopped crying, stood up, smoothed the crinkles out of her baby doll pyjamas (for that's all she was wearing), blew Henry a kiss, and left. Henry smiled to himself, much taken with his own kindness. 'I can forgive and forget,' he said.

Wendy was grumpy when she arrived. 'What's the matter, darling,' cooed Henry sweetly. 'Don't you want to be here?' The tall girl with long red hair paced round the room for several minutes before she eventually spoke. 'Bloody hell,' she finally blurted out, 'look what they've made me wear!' Wendy stopped, snarled, stared down at herself in disgust, pulled at her 'shortie' nightdress with nervous fingers. Henry was sympathetic. He knew Wendy well, after all, they'd lived together for three years, knew her hatred of all things traditionally feminine. 'It doesn't look so bad,' he said soothingly. Wendy was unconvinced, delivering a short lecture on the women's movement to prove her point; angry, angry, angry. Henry was a little frightened. Where were all these old girlfriends coming from? Did he have to see all of them?

He looked across at the bedroom door. What was going on out there? What was the 'Land of Satin Dolls'? He wanted to ask Wendy how she'd arrived, but she was gone. Henry made to get out of the bed. He couldn't move his legs. He was paralysed from the waist down.

After Wendy came Heidi. After Heidi, the lovely Nancy. He sat up in bed transfixed, watched the procession of familiar females with an increasing sense of disaster. Where would it all end? It was as if he was close to a mysterious female paradise – or was it a limbo? All the girls, apart from Wendy, spoke highly of the place. It seemed you didn't have to die to gain admission.

It was a place of dreams, a reality of the head. 'It's O.K.,' laughed Nancy before she left. 'I don't like the nightgear, but the food and the freedom's very good.' Then the lights went out.

The city looked threatening in the feeble morning light; long lines of traffic howled and roared. The bed descended through the polluted city air. Henry twitched, shook his head, found he could move his legs again. He saw the roof of his house arriving closer, closer.

Back in his own bedroom he looked round fondly at the familiar scene, the old bruised sideboard, the Van Gogh prints, the tall wobbly wardrobe. Spreading out his arms he stretched like a big cat. He opened his mouth wide, prepared to let out a great sigh of relief, but nothing, silence.

His mouth appeared to be stuffed full of a material of some kind. He sat up, thrust his hand into the aperture, started to pull out the offending stuff. Nightdresses! Short, silky, satin, soft, damp, rolled into little balls. Two hours later he was still easing them out. He couldn't speak. He was disastrously late for work.

EXPECTATIONS

The mountains are watching me. It's raining hard. The rough road's a swamp. I have difficulty walking. The trees seems to have extra-long branches that whip and tear at my face. I want to rest. My guide seems to have left me. I stumble and wobble on. Then, from nowhere, my mother's voice:

'Mrs Wallingford told me the Asiatics are moving into Blower Street. I think it's a shame; such lovely houses. The garden's a mess. I've got nobody to do it for me. I need a strong man and a wheelbarrow. Did I tell you about Connie Featherstone? She's gone senile – finished up in an old folk's home holding a teddy-bear and talking about ants in her underwear. It's a tragedy. I hope I don't go like that. I talked to Caroline Bull on the phone yesterday. Nice girl. Do you remember her? Her father was a kitchen-porter at that Chinese restaurant they pulled down. Oh dear . . . She told me about the state of the kitchens. I don't know how they got away with it! I couldn't eat in one of those places if they paid me a fortune. I'm particular. I'm choosy . . .'

Brightness, calm. The rain stops. The hills light up: gold, blue, orange. My guide is back by my side offering me a long-sleeved pullover. I put it on. 'Better?' he inquires kindly. We continue walking, but slowly. Finally we stop beneath a huge apple tree. 'Rest,' says my guide. 'Listen.' It's my mother again:

'I told Fred Arnold his bread was stale. My God, was he angry? I nearly called the police. I'm not a troublemaker, but I like things to be right. I met Alice Waldron on the way back from church. She was sympathetic. She said she never trusted his rolls. I said the jam in his doughnuts didn't bear thinking about. I watched the television when I got back to the house. It was one of those French films, people moving in and out of bedrooms. I didn't understand it. I switched it off till the news came on.'

I'm falling asleep. I can hear my mother snoring. The sun's out and some apple blossom has just dropped on my navel. My guide's stroking my brow with his wings, inducing happy thoughts. A voice. My father's this time:

'Life's all expectations, son. I used to worry about everything but not now. I've found a regular job helping people. There's so much trouble in the world, you don't know you're born! When it's all over you realize. It's confusing at first, but you soon learn the ropes, soon learn to knuckle down. You're busy, but relaxed. The walls fall down and the fresh air pours in. It's hard to describe. It's not your time yet.'

Am I really asleep?

Journey

ARTAUD AT BREAKFAST

Artaud sat down to breakfast. It was just after the war – the second one. I watched his jaws moving. There were crumbs all over the place. He didn't seem able to control his mouth.

I looked into his eyes (he didn't appear to mind), searched for the details inside his head, looked for moving pictures. I saw remarkable things: horses and carriages, guns with wings, enamel-faced generals screeching out orders. I was witness to a pageant.

The waiter had taken a dislike to Artaud. I sought to protect him, smiling and gesturing support with a croissant-filled right hand. He pretended not to notice. He bowed his head, dipped his hand into the basket of bread, moved it around wildly. I think he thought I'd come to take him away again. His paranoia was famous – I chose to ignore it.

Then it began, a resonant mental contact, booming, bouncing, echoing. I concentrated. He talked of a man called Phillip who owed him money, describing his pock-marked face in vivid detail. He lectured on about Marat, his mother, and a Parisienne witch called Simone. He loved detail, innuendo, facile asides. He was more amusing than I could ever have imagined. I felt his eyes blinking, switching moods on and off. It was if he was re-inventing knowledge. His words fell from the air, luxuriant, life-giving.

The sun shone, the waiters brought out huge red and yellow

umbrellas. Artaud drank cup after cup of coffee, smacking his lips, scratching occasionally at his pallid, tormented face. My eyes fixed on the crumbs around his feet (I couldn't stop them, they swivelled then stopped in two distinct movements), saw nuggets of pure gold. I opened my mouth in wonder, the spirit of Jonah tumbled in.

He got up to leave, spun round slowly, held on to the table for support. I wondered if I should follow him. After all, he had miracles to share, a familiar road to travel.

THE NAME-DROPPER

Did I ever tell you about the time I met George Bernard Shaw? What a character, not at all like his public image. He was a terrific boozer – very fierce. I met him on a train going from Crewe to Northampton. We talked about books and plays. The journey went by quickly (with the help of his bottle of Scotch). It was really interesting.

And then there was H.G. Wells. Did I ever tell you about him? What a coincidence. We were both at Moira Pilkington's birthday party; both a bit pissed, and we *both* went for the same girl. There was quite a scuffle. Dave Lawrence had to pull us apart. Still, it all worked out in the end. She told us she didn't want either of us and to stop wrestling on the carpet. I don't know, the things one does for love.

Who am I then? Do you want to know? If not – why not? No, joking apart, my name's David Lloyd George, not *the* David Lloyd George, but I'm a bloke with the same name. I was a postman by profession, although I was trained as a chimney-sweep before the bottom fell out of that. I'm getting a bit old now, but I've got my memories. Want to know about Ernest Hemingway and the time we played cards with Segovia? Oh, what a brawl that turned out to be! It's a wonder old Seggi could do his concert after that business. My wife wouldn't believe me when I got home, said I was making it all up.

My wife's wonderful, a relative of Dame Nellie Melba, the

Australian opera singer. I'd like to go 'down under'. Perhaps I'd meet that actor Rod Taylor again. Ever heard of him? He was in Hitchcock's *The Birds* with Nellie Melba. We got sozzled together in Malaya. I remember his parting words: 'If I ever see your ugly pommie face again I'll kick it in.' No, he was a good man really.

What am I doing now – at this moment? Do you want to know? I'm looking out of the window and – guess what – do you know who's just walking up the garden path? Joseph Stalin – old nasty Joe. I wonder what he wants? Wants to borrow my hedge-clippers again; he's so rough with them. He hasn't been round for some while. I suppose the wife will let him in.

Talking of visitors: Margaret Rutherford was round a few weeks ago. Oh, she has aged. I told her to liven her ideas up or her future in films would be in grave doubt. I don't know whether she took any notice. She had that Boris Karloff with her. What a nice man. A perfect charmer. My wife was so impressed; he knew more about baking apple tartlets than she did! He could have been a housewife in another existence. O.K., that's about it.

Oh, someone's tapping on the door. Who is it, Vanessa? Is it Joseph? Ah, come in old mate. Got the clippers have you? What's that you've got in your hand. Oh dear, I think you better put it away. It looks like a gun. Now Joseph, calm down. Vanessa! Vanessa! Bring some tea up and my signed copy of *Das Kapital*. Ah that's better, comrade. Oooh you gave me quite a shock. That's it, put it back in your shopping bag. Now then, let's be sensible. How's the roses coming on? Big tomatoes this year?

Trouble

SOLO

I'm solo, tied forever to the rhapsody of life – free. I have a few outstanding relationships, a few adventures. There's Phyllis and Doris and Dora and Davinia. There's Claudette and Clara and little Colleen Brown. I get around. I circulate. I live close to the centre of the city and drive a small black sports car. I ask no questions and attempt to tell no lies. I'm a furniture salesman, one of the best. I'm an expert where tasteful living-rooms are concerned: I've a lot of experience. Did I ever want to marry?

Difficult to say. I was engaged at nineteen to a rather pretty country girl: it didn't work out. Her father was a devout Christian and was forever making surprise appearances in the living-room when we were alone together. I used to get very annoyed. Nothing much happened. We split up on my twentieth birthday after a row over a motor-cycle. I'll never forget the day; it was wet and windy and she pushed me into a holly-bush. I can still hear the torrent of abuse.

So now I'm solo, thirty-four, and taking on the world. Am I attractive? Some would say so. My mother always said I was, 'The sheik of the family'. She loved me. She died two years ago from cancer of the throat. I cried a lot, so much that my girlfriend of the time (Colleen Brown) said it was unnatural. I was hurt. I left her outside the cinema and never spoke to her again. We were going to see a French film starring Jean-Paul Belmondo as a rebel. I never got to see it.

It's good being solo. I don't find it lonely. I've got a nice little flat and do all my own cooking. I'm a big television fan and normally visit some of the more select city bars at the weekend. I get around. I can do it. I'm capable. My best friend Garth Fox says he envies my lifestyle. 'You're such a lucky swine,' he says sometimes. I think I am. I'm sure I am. I know I am.

Will I ever tie the knot – get married? It's open to question. All I know is Brenda Wheeler is coming round tonight for a spot of slap and tickle.

She's very independent – a nurse. We've been seeing each other for two weeks now. All these women . . . Does it really make me a sheik? I miss my mother. The best there was. She used to ride on the back of my motor-cycle. I wished I could find someone as sporting and as lively as her. You never know. Pigs have been known to fly. I can wait.

AEROPLANES AND WOLVES

It seemed that the wolves were never far away. He heard aeroplanes when there were no aeroplanes. His older brother called it paranoia, said there was nothing to be afraid of. He believed him and didn't believe him. 'If they come,' (said a friend) 'we'll show them what's what.'

Who were the wolves? Were they encountered every day on the London underground? At his door? It was dreadfully hard to tell. His kitchen and toilet were stacked with old newspapers and magazines. 'My insurance,' he would say if asked about their purpose.

And insurance? Did it include the rabbit's foot hanging outside the bathroom window? Did it include the mystic Indian signs chalked on his letterbox? Insurance was necessary . . . it seemed.

He often talked about work, but never appeared to do any. He talked of poetry, writing hymns, and inventing a new musical instrument. 'It's got to be loud,' he would say (meaning the instrument), 'something to scare the shit out of the wolves.'

I talked to him a lot that summer. His fantasy helped to pass the time. His brother would make faces over his shoulder, try to make me laugh. I thought it cruel and unnecessary. His brother said he cared, but I had my doubts. Why did he tie his legs with wire at night? Why did he continually smack him about the head when he was eating? 'It stops him talking about wolves and aeroplanes,' he said when I asked him.

PURGATORY

I'm a glutton for pain, for gazing into the heavy eyes of nowhere. I dream of fibrositis, of a clinging, stinking, cancer. I never mention happiness. If I did, and I never ever will, I'd have to describe pink baby clothes and a house close to the woods – a touch of the Hansels and Gretels.

I might ask, if he'd allow, the man next to me to explain his wearing of a tweed cap. 'Would it be a present from the wife,' I might say. I can't though. I'm perfectly alone, without friend or possible accomplice.

But you could imagine it couldn't you, the silly cap flying through the air – landing on a pile of rotting sausages? It would have to be removed. It would have to be plucked from the head. How pleasant to envisage the resulting argy bargy, the weedy calls of protest.

I've thought of purchasing a stereo record player, something beefy and bold, something to galvanize the timid neighbours into unseemly protest. What a fine thing it would be to find them dressing-gowned and slippered complaining at my door. I'd like to see that grotesque bank clerk and his flat-chested wife up in arms. Who do they think they are with their politely tutored hairdo's, their pointed squeaky shoes?

This building stinks, there's something foul in the cellar. A plastic bag stuffed with offal perhaps? Whatever happened to the landlord's wife? I remember her last summer bending to unblock a drain. Such a bony arse – no substance, no character. When she stood up she took on the appearance of a bemused mother hen.

I'm reaching out, touching the frayed cuffs of an old jacket. Oh for the ability to stitch and sew, to make good the decrepit. I've heard it said that I'm a disgrace to the neighbourhood, that I lower the tone. What about Anderson, Fulgate, Priddle and Harry Boulder? Their presence in the public park is hardly a treat for the eyes. And their women? What about Ragged Norah, Dirty Alice? I can see them all now, cavorting, dribbling, lounging idly amidst the empty bottles. I've never reduced myself to that. I eat and drink at home.

I have to prove to myself that I exist, that I'm not simply a vague sliver of sour smelling atmosphere. I have needs beyond the realms of my independently financial status. There are many who imagine I'm satisfied, and who am I to disillusion them? Well, the fact is, I'm sufficiently an individual to want to do so.

Why should I deny myself the regalia of an important being? I'm always reading in newspapers about the security offered by an army career, about the spiritually fulfilling daily obligations of a postman.

I've composed numerous letters, sent telegrams, postcards, detailed lists of my personal accoutrements. I've mentioned the peculiar size of my waistcoat and trousers in an attempt to persuade the authorities of the seriousness of my intent. I want them to know my all, to be familiar with every aspect of my being.

But I suffer. Could I put it any plainer? A finality akin to hopelessness causes my shoulders to drop. And the reason? It's difficult to pin-point the cause. My mother has a strong personality, overweight and overbearing she was partial to large dinners and smacking me about the head shouting: 'Peas, eat your bloody peas.' I was often confused, divided between love and pure hate. My father was her complete opposite, a meek little man, enormously rich, but disastrously soft-hearted. 'It'll all work out,' he used to mutter, struggling to soothe me after one of my mother's periodic assaults. He was a lily-livered old swine.

I try to be positive; positively sad, positively stressed. Considering everything, as I always do, my attention to detail is pretty remarkable. I enjoy my pain, but never speak of enjoyment. I'm a man of military precision without any trace of military bearing. I dress shabbily, but distinctively. I'm broad of girth, but slim enough to wiggle through the holes in the fence at the back of the building. I'm often spoken of as a man of terrific willpower. Carlos came last night – Carlos my long-suffering spirit guide. We talked for an hour about the state of play in an other world. 'Eetz a mess up there,' he kept saying. He looked terribly ill. His matador suit was grubby, and his curly hair was noticeably unwashed. I found comfort in his appearance, proof of the humanness of the other side. Carlos confirmed the routine of it all.

What a change from his first visitation. If I remember rightly he wore a pair of purple trousers and a startling pair of translucent blue wings. He's calmed down over the years, realizing that reality rather than show is what I need. I'm grateful though. It's pleasing to know we don't just rot in the ground.

Oh, there's the doorbell. I wonder who it could be? There's a list of possibilities a mile long. What if it's Agatha from number forty-one?

She's amazing, likes to dress up in a fairy outfit and convince me she's just arrived to escort me to never-never land. Shall I answer? I might – I might not.

Terence is arriving after supper, wants to talk about fibrositis and renewing my subscription to the Labour Party. I keep busy, I see no end in the foreseeable future.

VICAR

Tombstone vicar with hair flapping into his eyes – nearly reaching his arse – nearly blocking up his mouth. Yes, he talks too much. He's noisy. The world knows it. Underground, the bones move, the skeletons walk. Grass grows up the signpost. It's a sight for dead eyes. The vicar should win the prize for the biggest cock in history. It substitutes as a tongue. It's sore. It *will* be sore. Help! The skeletons are dancing – fumbling with each other in the aisles. They must marry and make everything above board. It's a straightlaced world. Tie up the corset!

BAIRNSWORTH

I think it was the day he started to read the complete works of Marcel Proust: I took note of his behaviour. Of course I'd been studying him some time (far longer than he realized), but that was by the way. I'd been waiting for something to pin on him. I was grateful for the chance to strike. 'Bairnsworth,' I said, in my best authoritarian voice, 'isn't it time you stopped shilly-shallying and got down to basics?' Bairnsworth looked up from his Proust, fiddled with his repulsive round glasses, and farted. 'What do you mean?' he asked. I was completely deflated.

I could talk about Bairnsworth for hours. He tested my patience and tolerance more than any man I ever met. I see myself as the down to earth type; no nonsense, reliable. He thought of himself as an intellectual, a cut above the usual clerical officer. Nobody liked him. He didn't fit in. We all resented the fact that he ate his sandwiches in the boiler-room, that he refused to eat them at his desk like the rest of us.

Bairnsworth said he was a socialist. I thought he was more of a communist. His ideas for social reform were terrifically extreme (lots of nationalization and excessive health benefits) and his use of bad language was a pain. I hated it. I wanted it stopped.

How do you deal with a rebel in the office, an eternal teenager in his fiftieth year? Terry Widdowsen (our supervisor) was always trying. 'Keep the language down,' he'd shout:

'Button your lip!' It didn't work. Cyril Cardew (our deputy supervisor) attempted physical violence: it was a failure. Bairnsworth was strong, deceptively tough for his size.

John Frederick Bairnsworth was killed on the fourteenth of February nineteen eighty seven. His death occurred shortly after six thirty in the evening. It was a frightening business. I felt guilty about it afterwards. It's hard to forget the death of a colleague (even a Bairnsworth) especially when you could have possibly prevented it.

The platform of Clapham Common underground station was busy the night he died; trains were delayed, there were reports of a signal failure at Kennington. It was the usual nonsense. There were five of us, all going home: Cardew, Widdowsen, Shelton (a junior clerk), Bairnsworth, and myself. The conversation was fragmented but seemed to centre mainly around the fortunes of Chelsea football club. Bairnsworth (who hated all competitive sports) refused to join in. We all thought this rather typical, and ignored him.

Then it happened: a mob of skinheads pushed past shouting racist slogans; elbowing, pushing, kicking. Bairnsworth retaliated. It was a nightmare.

Have you ever seen a man trodden into the ground, jumped on until his body became an unrecognizable bloody pulp? That's what happened to Bairnsworth. The incident lasted approximately five minutes. We were all petrified, none of us lifted a finger to help him. I told my girlfriend about it in the pub later. 'You hated him,' she snorted unsympathetically: 'What are you so worried about?'

Isn't it funny how death brings people together? The day after Bairnsworth died (reports talked of a fractured skull), Cardew organized a collection for a wreath. I contributed a fiver. 'Cheap at the price,' muttered Cardew, a half-smile on his face as he tucked my offering into his wallet. Hard words? I don't think so. I remembered Bairnsworth's sense of humour; it was pretty black at times. I think he would have approved.

DEAD POET

1

'I think I've got it wrong,' he said. 'There has to be a bit better life than this.' We all frowned, made faces, yawned. He wasn't so far from the river then.

The thing I remember most of all was his glasses. I think he stuck them together with sticking plaster till they finally fell apart – just before he jumped, into the river that is. A snotty child found them, put them over his tiny nose. A news photographer took a picture of him. It was a creepy shot, the child holding them together with chubby hands.

I joined the therapy group three years ago (I think they call them 'self-help' groups now). We met in the community hall. Our group used to get together after the pregnant mothers meeting. It was a lively gathering (apart from our friend with the broken glasses). We all thought it a tonic to be there. I vividly remember a Tuesday evening when our short-sighted friend read us one of his poems. It was a desultory piece about winter in the inner-city. There was a brief protest before he started. One of the group (an insomniac lorry driver) called out, 'oh, not again.' I was taken aback. It seemed unnecessary, nothing to do with the optimism of our gatherings. Anyway, he read the poem and it was utterly, dumbfoundingly, depressing. One could hear a mass sigh of relief after he'd finished. Our poet left early, refusing the usual cup of tea and biscuit afterwards. He was undoubtedly upset.

For some years I was subject to crippling depression; foul, bleak days when everything collapsed around me. I took pills, consulted analysts, tried meditation: nothing really worked. The therapy group saved my sanity. It was comforting to know there were others in the same boat as myself. I made new friends.

2

It's approaching winter, and I'm not looking forward to it. The scene in my garden is one of threatened catastrophe. I can see hungry little birds cowed by the onset of the cold; dying flowers, naked and humiliated trees. There's a noticeable change in the behaviour of my fellow human beings. People scowl at their neighbours on public transport, mutter to themselves about the petty faults of others. There's a marked lack of tolerance. I witnessed a fight in the public library recently. I didn't join in. Who wants to squabble over the latest John le Carré? It's the weather; it stimulates these silly conflicts.

I'm hoping to avoid flu this winter. I've stocked up with boxes and boxes of suitable medication. I'm unemployed at the moment so I don't meet many germ carriers. I think office work can be a risky business at this time of the year. What about all those people sneezing in confined spaces? I'm looking for outdoor work; gardening, something like that. I've always taken an interest in plant life. I like to watch things grow.

I left the therapy group some time ago. I think there's a time when therapeutic activity loses its purpose: after all, who wants to listen to some self-pitying widower talking about his sexual difficulties every other night, or some old biddie cackling on about her constipated cats? It got boring. I started to go to the cinema more regularly.

I was talking on the phone to my mother recently. She asked me if I'd found another girlfriend. Why does she always ask the same question? What's wrong with being forty-five and free? I'm always telling her I'm perfectly content, but she doesn't believe me. I think that this is the most interesting time of my life.

3

A letter arrived this morning from the sister of the poet with the broken glasses. It was a total surprise. I had no idea she knew where I lived. The letter was all about suicide, how he'd thrown himself off Hammersmith Bridge. She wrote that he thought I was 'a very sympathetic person'. It seems odd. I only spoke to him three times.

Suicide's not the best of solutions. I read somewhere that if you kill yourself you're: 'Destined to exist in eternity within a grey translucent cloud.' If it's true it isn't worth it. I've never contemplated suicide: never!

Thinking back, I wonder if the group could have helped him more? We were unkind to him. Would things have been different if we'd applauded his poem? It's stupid to speculate. He was a miserable bastard really.

TWILLING'S TRAGIC AFFAIR

1

His memory starts THEN. He rubs his thumb and forefinger together to stimulate the required sensation. It doesn't stretch his brain too far to imagine that certain day in 1946. His mind touches imitation silk (showy but impractical) savouring the sensuality. And so it is. And so you bear with him as he relates each pin-prick of existence. You are asked to be patient.

They chide the romantic these days. He hides his personal thoughts. 'Do you hear voices?' they ask trying to vanquish the inner call. They deny God. They deny him the right to speak.

He clearly recollects the first time God had a word with him. He's got an excellent memory. 'It was in 1946,' he says.

1946 was a memorable year: The war has just ended, luxuries were scarce, chocolate tasted better then. If he sucks in deeply, concentrates, he can see his little pink mouth rimmed with chocolate stains. 1946 was the year that his senses first started to work.

2

It's autumn, getting cold. Twilling, friend of our romantic friend, is offering sympathy on the telephone. 'Of course God made you,' he's saying as he struggles to balance a cup of tea on the arm of the settee, 'of course he did.' He puts the telephone down gently, releases a long tortured sigh of frustration. 'He isn't getting any better,' he complains. Karin laughs. Much later, after an unusually intense discussion of the day's news, the engaged couple part. 'If we were married we wouldn't need to do this,' she almost hisses as she snuggles against his shoulder. Twilling is practising caution; he was caught out once before. Karin takes her leave. 'Mustn't forget my umbrella,' she says anxiously, racing back to the lounge.

It's three o'clock on a Sunday morning, the telephone rings. 'Who is it?' Twilling asks, half knowing the answer. The caller doesn't reply, simply asks (in that familiar tearful voice), 'Does Jesus really love me?' Twilling reaches for his cigarettes. 'Of course he does,' he answers reassuringly. The caller rings off. It's an annoying process. How far can one push friendship before it finally collapses? Twilling shuffles to the kitchen. 'I feel like a bloody wet rag,' he grumbles loudly.

Early Sunday evening; Twilling's well-appointed home's choked with cigarette smoke. 'Did he ring again?' asks Karin. Twilling pauses, holds his breath momentarily. 'Yes,' he answers, 'twice.' 'Perhaps we should pop round to see him,' says Karin. As she speaks two drunks can be heard arguing in the street below, the words 'fuck' and 'cunt' repeated over and over again. 'Is the window open?' Twilling asks. Karin smiles. 'Never could stand the rougher element could you?' she comments.

3

Twilling's got a heart of solid gold; a practising Christian, he's never been known to reject a needy case. He's reasonably well off, almost prosperous. His flat, modern, functional, homely, is situated in the rich heart of the city. Famous for his compassion

– as well as for his bursts of foul temper – he's a man with many friends.

Wednesday evening, and Twilling's preparing to lock up his antique shop. He looks around slowly, savouring the details of his property with a loving eye. It was a good investment, the complete antidote to the insecurity of old age. The telephone suddenly chirps into life. He picks it up, tucks the receiver between his shoulder and chin, talks. 'Yes,' he half blusters. 'What can I do for you?' a voice wheedles, whimpers. 'Did Jesus really die for me?' it asks. It's too much, there's a point where religious mania starts to grate. 'I don't fucking know!' Twilling shouts, slamming the phone down, aiming a kick at the overflowing wastepaper basket.

4

The caller drops the receiver, it clatters noisily across the bare wooden floor! 'Twilling,' he yells, 'you two-faced NOTHING!' Then he starts to cry. It's unbearable, Twilling was the last one to care. What can Jesus do for him now? His memory's failing. Did he go to work recently? He doesn't remember. He lifts himself slowly, wearily, from the unmade bed, carefully avoids the corpse of his female friend. 'Why did you have to come round?' he yells, baring his teeth, foaming at the mouth, 'why?' He was happy with Karin once; she was his girl.

Now he's standing at the open window, calmer, watching a neighbour empty his rubbish into the vast, black, communal bin. Should he jump out or call for help? It's all so futile. Jesus isn't talking. Should he ring Twilling back, tell him what happened, tell him how Karin came round with some groceries, and he killed her?

5

Twilling's home, dog-tired but satisfied with life. It isn't very often he takes positive decisions. He consoles himself, if he needs consoling, with a large brandy. Why couldn't his romantic friend accept that he'd lost Karin, that she preferred the love of a secure and capable man to a dreamer? He kicks off his shoes, drops into an easy chair. Karin's due about nine o'clock. She didn't ring at the shop. He imagines her flustered, queueing at a public telephone box, unable to get through. He falls asleep smiling. He's really in love.

WEDDING NIGHT

1

It was the panorama from a dream; gilded rooftops, lacquered spires, towering columns of light. They stood on the slippery white-tiled balcony, clutched hard at sleek ebony rails. 'We won't fall, will we?' she asked, undisguised terror in her little-girl voice. 'No,' he replied, imbuing himself with a new masculine firmness. 'It's all as it should be; we can stay here forever.'

Their hotel room was lavishly (but tastelessly) decorated. It was a disappointment. The view from the balcony, however, was more than adequate compensation. She tested the bed; bouncing up and down, up and down. 'It's lovely,' she chirruped. 'Don't make so much noise,' he called angrily from the bathroom. 'They might be listening.' She stopped suddenly and chuckled to herself: his paranoia was a joke.

They fell asleep just before midnight. He was happy; all his fears about their honeymoon vanquished after a satisfying sexual encounter. 'That was wonderful,' she murmured before she turned off her bedside lamp. He was pleased with himself. It had been worth the irritating wait. They were an old-fashioned couple. Marriage was something sacred.

He was woken at four o'clock in the morning by a loud buzzing sound. He sat up straight. What was it? It was too cold for insects, and anyway, they didn't make that much noise. 'Who's there?' he called in a trembling voice. 'What do you want?' As his eyes grew accustomed to the darkness he was startled to see the figure of a man standing by the open balcony window. 'Who the hell are you?' he demanded above the buzzing. 'What are you doing here?' The man moved swiftly forward, leaned over the bed, produced a gleaming metal saw from behind his back. 'I've come to saw your bride in half,' he said, spitting out his words with relish. 'I've come to split the difference.' Within seconds the husband was out of the bed grappling with the stranger. His bride woke up. 'Is it breakfast time?' she asked in a sleepy voice. The two men wrestled in the half light. The bee-like buzz of the saw whined to a halt. 'He's out cold,' yelled the husband from the bedroom floor. 'I think I've knocked him out.' It had been a brief but conclusive fight. The bride turned on the bedroom light. 'Is it a burglar?' she inquired. She was wonderfully calm.

2

Dismembering a tall muscular human is a difficult task. The couple spent two days making a reasonable job of it. 'I didn't know I was that strong,' complained the husband during a tea-break (the knock-out blow had proved fatal). 'Perhaps Ernest had a weak heart,' said his bride, a worried look on her chubby face. 'What a honeymoon!' he exclaimed. 'We must do some sightseeing when this is all over.' They needed some fresh air and good food; existing on bad room-service had started to become depressing.

When the work was completed and parts neatly wrapped up (in pieces of his corduroy dressing gown) they felt a new and powerful sense of companionship flood over them. This wasn't some sickly ice-cream relationship, all lovey-dovey and sloppy kisses. They were together forever in the deepest possible way.

They had real secrets to keep.

It was almost full moon when they threw Ernest's remains off the balcony. 'It's a good job the oriental pond is just below our room,' whispered the bride as she tossed a leg into the night air. 'I hope there's enough weight in these parcels. I hope they sink properly.' 'Don't worry,' he replied, voice crammed with confidence. 'I think this is the last we'll see of that old boyfriend of yours.'

Jealousy's a nasty emotion. Why (they wondered) had her old lover trailed them to their honeymoon hotel, climbed the four storeys to their room, and attempted to cut her in half with a saw? 'I don't think he ever got over the time I left him in that tea-shop near Euston station,' she mused. 'Funny though,' she continued, reaching for the telephone to order a taxi to take them out to a local nightspot: 'I had a feeling he wasn't any ordinary madman as soon as you started to take that silly mask off his face.'

It was approaching midnight. The couple stood on the balcony looking out across the beautiful city. The busy landscape glowed and twinkled. They could hear the distant exciting sound of a Latin American band. An exquisite silence filled the hotel garden, disturbed only by the laughing quack-quack of a lonely duck on the oriental pond.

THE LAST OF MAUREEN

Before they took her out she spoke of aniseed balls, a rampaging elephant, an ill-fated husband.

Her stockings – wrinkled – dripped dangerously close to the wet clay. I heard them ask if her coat was warm enough (as if it really mattered!). I didn't hear what she said at the time.

That night, I dwelt upon the contents of her mind. Did she really deserve to die so ingloriously? I saw a frosty terrain, narrow ill-lit streets, a tiny kitchen window, cracked and filthy glass. I saw her round painted face looking out, saw the shadow of her dreams like Disney cartoon figures on crumbling bedroom walls. She'd come so far. Why had it got so out of hand?

It seemed, they said, that she'd always craved for more than her fair share of everything; talked often, as a schoolgirl, of palaces, spacious apartments, a rich and generous husband. The general verdict on her personality was that she was 'Pushy and ruthless – always ambitious.' I detected jealousy in their voices, but her history seemed to confirm the judgement. She'd come a long way from the small town of her birth.

The north never appealed to me; the brazen misuse of the English language failed to captivate. I was never charmed. 'So hoity toity,' they would say on my infrequent visits. I felt no shame. Maureen – for that was the name of the woman they 'disposed' of – was from the north.

It was an amazing career. If anyone had told me that a part-time barmaid could rise to the most influential position in the land I would have called them dreamers, but she did it. She did it with the cunning misuse of matriarchal power. She did it while the nation watched, did nothing. She was always being interviewed on TV. It was ridiculous. She used to wear expensive low-cut dresses, high heels, impossibly vulgar mini-skirts. I couldn't stand the sound of her northern vowels. I loathed the dropped aitches, the smutty slang. I felt sorry for her interviewers. They tried to be polite, but they suffered. She took pleasure in belittling their accents, always reminding them of her humble origins. With winks at the cameramen she'd interrupt their flow, make mockery of serious discussion. She had the power and she used it. She was as common as dirt.

It was a corrupt government. The people nearly starved while the leaders ate from golden plates. It was difficult to buy a decent piece of bacon, impossible to trust the meat pies. There was an eternal energy crisis. It was almost always dark in winter. The leaders built palaces, country houses, ugly monuments to the regime. Humour was at a premium. I didn't share a joke with anyone for years.

When she married the prime minister we all had a day off work. It was described as a 'magnificent idea' by the papers, 'a love match to end all other love matches.' The truth was something different. Within weeks she was pulling strings, turning the country into a land of nosey-parkers and gossips. You couldn't trust your neighbour anymore. Their photograph (smiling—holding hands) was on display everywhere. No one defaced it. It was a serious crime to even try.

She instigated novel projects, was obsessed with long-term planning. The people seemed to like her, called her 'The mother of all,' and 'Our great visionary.' She arranged for the weekly

45

distribution of aniseed balls to every child under eight years of age. A dentist who protested was sent to prison for fifteen years. 'Mother knows best,' was the opinion of the masses.

After ten catastrophic years the prime minister and his wife were deposed. There was a takeover led by a group of military men – revolutionary slogan: 'Down with petticoat government.'

The new leadership was very much like the old, but with one exception; the prime minister was a bachelor, a former general who collected model trains. We endured ten wasted years, ten years under the heel of a senile male and a bullying female. It was a waste of public money. What the hell happened? And their children? What a farce. I was insulted when the whole country was made to watch their youngest son playing foot-ball with a baby elephant on TV. 'It's his special treat,' they told us.

I could go on. There were 'starvation weeks', weeks when the public were forced to fast in order to pay for some new monument or other. There were 'Kiss Mummy and Daddy days' when the people were forced to wait in line to kiss placards of the prime minister and his wife. There were 'Mummy's little gifts', schemes like the aniseed ball nonsense, designed to curry favour with children. Sad to say, it seemed to work. The country wanted dictators. The people respected the police and the army. I was considered to be 'a public nuisance' for voicing my views. They put me in prison four times.

Her husband died first, trampled to death by the baby elephant. Maureen was shot two hours later.

Everyone remarked how old she looked in the end, much older than her forty-five years. The palace grounds were an unnerving sight, the lawn strewn with looted dresses and shoes, her corpse by a fountain, mouth agape. 'What did she say when you asked her if her coat was warm enough?' I asked the officer in charge afterwards. 'Oh,' he replied, his face blossoming into a smile, 'something like,' and he tried to imitate her coarse voice, 'mind your own business you cheeky young sod.'

I shivered. That had to be Maureen, charming to the last.

COMPLAINT

I used to know him. I knew him before she knew him. He didn't listen when I said I knew him. He should listen. Why? He should. There's no *why*! He should.

THE PARTING

'Life's very pernicious', she said as she turned to walk back into the kitchen. I was praying at the time, my head thrust into a pile of dusty cushions. 'I need a vision,' I called – 'something a little special.' I don't think she heard me.

That evening I arrived late for the cinema. 'Curses,' said a fellow latecomer with a moustache. 'Shall we go ten-pin bowling,' I asked him – 'Instead?' We went looking for the place but failed to find it. 'She looks like a fallen angel,' remarked my companion, as we passed an old woman wearing a police helmet. The city was black and silent. 'I wish I had my camera,' he said. It was a deep baritone voice, unusual for a man with his size of head. I told him and he roared with laughter. 'Wonderful, wonderful', he shouted, crushing a cigarette end into the pavement.

'Where the hell of you been!' she called as I opened the front door. I found it difficult to answer immediately as my mouth was stuffed with roast-beef sandwich (a gift from a late-night reveller). 'Are you dumb or something,' she called again. I decided on silence and retired to the settee with a book. I heard the rustle of the silk eiderdown and muffled curses but I refused to be intimidated. We were drifting apart.

I was late for the factory the next day. My legs were lead tubing, the pedals wouldn't move properly on my bicycle. Somebody yelled 'late again', as I wobbled through the main gates. I nearly cried. It wasn't fair. I blamed it on the relationship with my female companion of the last twenty years. Were we suited to each other?

'Life's a bramble bush,' she said as she dusted my cap. 'What's the matter?' I inquired. 'Why so friendly tonight?' She didn't answer. I suspected trouble. I was nervous. It had been a difficult day at work.

There was nothing much on the television. We talked a little, mainly about our Chinese neighbours and the price of cauli-flowers. When I retired that night I was surprised to find the bed full of pots and pans.

'What's this!' I called, removing a frying pan from my pillow. I heard the door slam and footsteps down the garden path. It was the final straw. I went downstairs to the kitchen to make a cup of tea and discovered my truss and underpants crammed into the gas oven. Symbolic?

I wasn't sure. I thought of the old woman in the policeman's helmet. It cheered me up for the rest of the evening.

A CITY MAN

Timid, he set forth on to the London underground passing, without so much as a nod or little wink, skinheads diving for pennies, over-zealous staff licking away graffiti with their tongues. In the carriage he thrust his head into a paper bag with holes in it; a special move designed to avoid contact with fellow passengers. The woman in the next seat was counting money loudly. He smelt the breath. It was garlic again. In his mind he played gods and goddesses, inhabited a land dotted with hot-dog stands; well-muscled sales boys cajoled him into buying.

He was no duffer where loneliness was concerned. His frequent journeys through the bowels of the earth were perfect essays in how to avoid intimate relationships. He was a man of some bearing, some inherited pride. His stiffness was genetic. 'I come from that part of the universe where all natural desires are unfulfilled,' he would say. He was English.

Historians are a weird bunch (as are philatelists and professional pall-bearers): it's a recognized fact. They spend hours and hours in libraries, wear unflattering clothes, and are often too absorbed in research to change their underwear regularly. Our traveller was an historian – a lost but determined soul. His investigations into the origins of the Thirty Years War were renowned for their erudition, their brave scholarship.

His was a cluttered flat: assorted socks hung from a sagging clothes-line, books and maps rotted around the walls. The cooker needed cleaning, cups and saucers always required rinsing. His environment didn't bother him. He'd once had a girlfriend who'd insisted on cleaning up; she was given short shrift. He was a man without any colour sense. There were no pictures on the walls. In the bathroom, with its mildewed taps and cracked sink, hung his 'masks', the paper bags with eye and mouth holes. They were positioned over the mirror and were attached by string to long nails. They were his rudimentary but essential disguise. The thickness of paper was important; heavy brown bags made him sweat.

It was tea-time; a little ritual. He sat silently in front of a heaped plate of fish and chips, lifted his fork slowly, took the plunge. He ate greedily, noisily – little pieces of fish spurted from the corners of his mouth. It had been a long and hungry day in the public library; no cups of tea, no tasty snacks. At precisely eight o'clock he would enter the saloon bar of a nearby pub, order a cold pint of lager.

The youthful barman would ask the question he always asked: 'Going to wear the bag tonight?' The little crowd at the bar would laugh – they always did. He thought of making changes (the predictability of things was too much), but he couldn't. He was addicted.

It was a monstrosity of a pub, built when the pound was worth a pound, built to service the every whim of a dis-enchanted populace. It never seemed full: had it ever been? He sat in a corner underneath two tinted photographs of prize fighters. This was the most relaxing part of the day; he felt wonderful.

It was soon nine o'clock, time to put a bag on. With a quick nervous movement he took one from his overcoat pocket and placed it on his head. He folded his arms afterwards, acknow-ledged the small round of applause from the bar. 'Ignorant peasants,' he muttered under his breath. It was a curious sight:

the man in the overcoat with a bag on his head – the empty pint of lager at his right hand.

He was home by eleven. It was a warm sticky night, the kind of night he'd wished he'd taken a bus. It was short-sleeve weather.

He took his overcoat off, threw it on the back of a chair; took the bag off his head, hung it on a nail in the bathroom. He made some toast, spread it thickly with margarine and jam – munched loudly. It had been the usual kind of day. Would it always be so? Maybe one day the gigglers in the pub would turn against him, kick his head in for his strangeness? Maybe they'd ban him from the library for refusing to take the bag off his head while reading? There were many times when he felt a freak, a total outcast. He had identity problems – he knew it. Still, the big city understood – it had left him alone . . . up to now.

ANGEL

.

After the old artist was reborn he found himself on Streatham
High Road. There were a lot of new and strange things to see.
The clothes shops, with their life-like dummies, frightened him
a little. He liked the look of some of the food being sold, but
remembered he didn't need to eat. Heaven had proved to be a
miraculous place with fool-proof remedies for natural human
desires. He patted his stomach as he walked. He was slim. He
didn't eat, smoke, or get drunk (an abominable habit of his
youth). He was simply HERE, and enormously grateful to
be so.

He sat on a bench on Streatham Common. An old woman
quietly placed herself next to him. She was small with friendly
little eyes and nibbled politely at a ham sandwich. 'Gorgeous
weather we're having,' she said breezily between tiny mouth-
fulls. He nodded in agreement. He didn't speak as he wasn't sure
if he could. Silence was his favoured policy. 'Are you all right
dear?' she asked after a long silence. He nodded again, grinned
positively. She was sympathetic: with his wide-brimmed hat
and black velvet cape he looked dreadfully uncomfortable. It
was a hot day.

When he got up to leave she touched his arm. 'I should take
that heavy thing off,' she said, pointing to his cloak. He grinned
again. She was a concerned and caring human being but a bit of a
nuisance. He wanted to be left alone; there was so much he had

to see. He waved goodbye. He wanted to tell her how happy he felt. He was sorry he couldn't.

It was late afternoon and still warm. He was sitting under a tree watching a group of children playing. Two boys were kicking a football around. He felt soothed, sleepy, exceptionally calm. Then, without any apparent reason, they started to argue. The ball was suddenly forgotten, a fight began. The other children gathered round shouting, pointing. He thought about intervening. Heaven was different. He wasn't used to violence. 'Oh God above,' he heard himself praying, 'please make them stop.' The fight continued. God obviously didn't want it to stop. Perhaps a lesson was being learned? 'Fuck off Abbot,' he heard one of the boys shout as he hurried from the nasty scene. What did he mean, 'fuck off?' It sounded like the very worst kind of insult.

It was dark when he reached the bus shelter. He sat down stiffly on the scarred plastic seat. It was getting cold. He felt awkward: what on earth could he do next? He sat back, tried to relax, thought seriously about heaven. Would Reynolds still be telling his long boring stories when he got back? Would old Richmond still be washing his shirts in that brook at the back of the manor house? They all got on his nerves sometimes, but this – was it any better? He stared across at the fish and chip shop on the other side of the road, noted the crowd of short-haired young men squabbling with each other. He watched, nerves jangling, as a fat youth boarded a motorbike and kicked it noisily into life. It was beyond his comprehension: what was the point of such horrible machines? What were those things that people kept stuffing into their mouths? He decided it was time to leave.

As he climbed onto the roof of the bus shelter he lost a shoe. 'Curses,' he shouted, and was surprised. He could speak! His voice was as audible here as it was in heaven. He immediately felt terribly rude. It would have been nice to have exchanged a pleasantry or two with the old lady on the common.

A small crowd gathered. The words 'looney' and 'nut-case' were heard repeatedly. 'Whatever happened to the English language?' he called down as he dropped his cape and opened his big silver wings. Someone threw a handful of cold chips, they brushed past his chin as he prepared to leap.

It was a perfect night for ascent. The light from the moon was a gift. Far below a scraggy child picked up his abandoned shoe. He tore the silver buckle off. 'Could be useful,' he muttered; 'fucking silver – must be worth a few bob!'

BARFLY

Why are there so many problems? Ethiopia! What about that? Look, I tell you, there are times when everything gets too much. Mrs Finkle. Know her? She sits in her flat everyday like a divine rabbit. I told Mrs Sharon about her, whispered in her worldly ear. 'Mad,' she said. I can't stand the wailing through the walls. I call it collapsible reversitude. Know what it means? I don't.

The bar's rather full tonight. I like the look of that black man with the red shirt. What would we talk about if we got round to talking to each other? Ethiopia? I'm not qualified to talk about it. Who's that blonde he keeps laughing at? I've a jaded view of life. It's my upbringing.

I was touched by the holy spirit yesterday. It was something akin to my experience in the kitchen during the hot summer of 1959. I was talking to the newspaper boy when – suddenly – I saw a white light over the geraniums. It seemed perfectly natural. I accepted it. I heard the sea. I thought I heard distant clarinets. I was roused from my reverie by the boy asking for his money. I remember noticing a hole in his socks as he left. He slammed the gate very hard.

This bar's a cosmopolitan bar, you get all types. I usually talk to Jack Crowson. He's an amiable soul, an old soldier. He tells some hair-raising stories. He's always yapping on about his bowel movements. I find him relaxing company most of the time, a change from the civil servants I usually mix with. Oh, wait a minute, here's Jack now:

All right Jack?
Not so bad.
What are you having to drink?
A pint of bitter please.
How's the back passage?
Playing up a bit – very sore.
Oh dear . . . sorry to hear it.

I've just passed Jack his pint over. He seems to be involved with old Herbert Fiddler. I can't stand him. He's very mean. They tell me he beats his wife as well. She is a nice person. Why doesn't she leave him?

I feel a burst of palpable pulverization coming on. It's hard to describe it. It's to do with Linda Hodges. She's just arrived with Cecil what's-his-name from the next village:

Hi Linda!
Hi Ernest!
What's in the wind tonight?
Ernest! Why should I tell you?
Well, because I like to know about your comings and goings...

Oh, she's moving away. Old what's-his-name doesn't seem to like me. Jealousy? She got my name wrong. She always does. She's beautiful – my dream. Why can't I find the right partner in life? Am I to be forever duped by facile fate? I have a picture in my head of the perfect housewife, a clean kitchen, porky sausages sizzling on a hot stove. I need love, warmth, a billion cuddles. I want a cottage with roses by the door. I need to hear sentimental love songs. Where can I find it all? My mother said I was destined to be unhappy. She was the last person to cook me a decent meal.

Ah well, it's nearly midnight. Time to go home. Home? What a laugh. A flat. A smelly little cesspit surrounded by more smelly little cesspits – a grubby cube of loneliness. Mrs Sharon says I need female companionship, don't wash my trousers regularly enough. 'Women have changed,' she says. I wished I could meet one to find out. Oh – hold on – there's Linda. She seems to be leaving:

Goodnight Linda.

Goodnight Edward.

Drive carefully dear.

I'll try . . . Goodnight.

My God, she remembered my name. Maybe she fancies me? My luck might be changing. I can feel a tingling in my unwashed socks. Fingers crossed. You never know.

MY FRIEND AND I

My friend and I are reluctant to talk about it. We've thought about it. Satisfied? No, I don't suppose you would be. I didn't expect it. We've changed over the years, developed a new pattern to our behaviour. We've finished with sparkling nights, silly seasons, barefoot runs through the midnight streets.

We live together. We're friends. We're sensible. We don't like a lot of fuss or a lot of noise. We're in a cocoon, well wrapped up. We talk in whispers. Can you hear me? It doesn't matter. Words are words. We know and we say so. We don't need to listen to anything.

My friend and I invite you to tea. We drink out of big cups. Our cake is very good. There's icing and cherries. The cream is real cream. Makes your mouth water. See the dribbles? There's cream on your moustache, tea-stains on your bosom. I can see her knickers when she bends over. Oh . . . Did you see that? Nice. The evenings are drawing in, filling us up with feelings of insecurity. We know. We've been here before. Close the curtains and keep the rain drops out.

My friend and I are mending a hole in the roof. We share most tasks. I help him with his homework and he helps me with my gardening. My cabbages are huge this year. No, no point in being flippant . . . they really are! People laugh at gardeners – laugh at their knowledge and their awareness. We have no friends. His homework is difficult.

The Vision

My friend and I are wrestling with a problem. What to do?
Where to go? Tunisia would be nice. Arab women with masks
on their faces? They don't like confusion. All the houses are
made out of mud – some are made out of marble.

It's somewhere to go – somewhere to hang your hat when it
rains.

DECLINE

He loved walking. Laughed a lot. Detested communism. Was prone to fantasies about being president of the USA. Was old-fashioned. The world was moving too fast for him.

The corner shop was full of spies. 'It's the weather, it changes his face,' commented an insensitive neighbour. He was middle-aged: 'A time of great doubt,' in the parish priest's opinion. It had been the hottest summer in Germany for several years.

That night, he prepared himself a soothing foot-bath. He had a theory that the warm water caused the blood to circulate more freely. 'It's clogged up,' he said to himself. As he sat soaking his feet he talked to the clock. 'You've got a friendly face,' he said.

The next morning he tripped over a bucket on his way to the outside toilet. On the way to the factory he slipped on a banana skin. His was a life of systematic futility.

Things changed after his election to chairmanship of the workers ice-hockey club. He decorated his house with trophies and pennants, took an active interest in skating boots. There was little time for illusion. Ice-hockey players are a tough breed.

He met Beryl at the Annual General Meeting. Beryl was a tall full-breasted woman five years younger than himself. They married after a six month courtship. Everyone at work and at the ice-hockey club thought them perfect for each other. They were right.

'I used to be such a fanciful bloke,' he said to Beryl one night over tea. 'Yes, you were,' she said, nodding in agreement. 'It's better now though.'

Then he went mad. It was near Christmas. He fell off his bike. It was icy and he was overloaded with parcels. In the hospital they said it was a case of 'mild bruising – nothing serious'. Beryl took him home and put him to bed. In the morning he was the president of the United States.

It was a good hospital. The Germans thought of everything Beryl, who (unlike her husband) spoke the language fluently was well satisfied with his treatment. 'When's Mao Tse Tung coming?' asked the invalid before she left.

He never got better. Beryl (after visiting him regularly for over two years) met and married a handyman from Saarbrücken. The visits stopped. He didn't notice.

Today he's alone. Makes great speeches by the hospital lake. He's regressed. 'I have a duty to perform,' he warns. It's unbearably sad. He speaks wisely for several minutes then falls asleep. The nurses take him inside for a rest. One of them smiles, pats his face. 'Achtung!' she shouts. The president sleeps, oblivious for a while. The affairs of state are often too tiring for him.

A WALK IN THE COUNTRY

Have you ever made love in a wheelbarrow, watched the beetles knocking their heads together through the cracks in the wooden boards? Have you stood in a country lane, been suddenly surprised by naked pink buttocks rising up and down in a nearby field? Erotic pleasures are few in my part of the world. Work always comes before pleasure. The life of a country schoolmaster can become sterile and stiff, especially if he's a poet as well.

So, here I am. It's Sunday and I've very little to do. I'm taking a long walk in an attempt to nullify the ravages of a stodgy dinner. It's August and the sun's shining. The birds are twittering madly, and voles are skidding beneath my brogues. I have few problems. I'm unmarried, almost forty-five, pleasantly well off. My hair's a little thin, but I'm certainly not bald.

Now, a decision. Should I climb the turnstile by Wilfred Harrison's smallholding, or should I carry on past Madge Slocum's and buy a bag of gooseberries? Decision made! I think I'll traverse the turnstile and cross into Halibut's wood. I'm glad I'm wearing such stout shoes, the rain was pretty heavy last night.

That was quick. It didn't take long. Oh, what's that sound? Twigs snapping. Somebody coming? Just a second; I know that face, that pert round bottom. It's Margaret Culsworth:

'Hi Margaret.'

'Hello Dick.'

'What are you doing out on your own? Don't you know there could be dangerous men about?'

Oh, she's ignoring me – walking off. What have I done to upset her? She's looking back now, sticking her tongue out. I thought she liked me.

I seem to have been walking for ages. I think I've over-stretched myself. My feet are starting to hurt. I must be getting old. What about that Margaret Culsworth? I thought she had respect for me, liked me. I put it down to too much liberal thinking, too much sex and familiarity with men. I prefer the old-fashioned type of young woman.

That's it then, time to walk back – retrace my weary steps. It's been an interesting afternoon. I've communed with nature, trod firmly on God's good earth.

Life can't be all exotica; sex in wheelbarrows, little pink bottoms rising in the moonlight. I've got my job, my cottage, the love and care of a good mother. I'm thankful. It's been an inspirational sort of day. I wonder where Margaret Culsworth went to? Perhaps she met her boyfriend on the way back to the village? They could be making love in one of Farmer Tibbet's barns. Perhaps I'll catch them at it. Perhaps they'll let me watch?

Europe 1387

MASSACRE

They lay in piles with their heads pointing at the gutter. There was a drunken man fiddling, buzzing over the bodies like a fly. There was no one to stop him. The cross-road was empty. No traffic. The lights remained on red.

A DAY IN THE LIFE OF A
GERMAN MYSTIC

I seek the divine, but the divine also seeks me. I would embrace him if he would let me, but my imagination makes a fierce ghoul of him, puts shadows under his eyes, adds an extra sharpness to his teeth. In his mysterious meditative state I'm able to call on saints, but I'm reluctant.

In this little room, by this surging river, by this green mountain, I feel compelled to make a statement. This pen, this mangy quill, has set itself another task. It's a merry scene outside; old Burckhardt foisting his lecherous intentions on Ursula, Müller drunk, playing skittles. I would participate if I could, but God has given me another duty.

So, a moment's thought, then to the bottom of it. I see, through the weed-ridden river so irritatingly put before my eyes, a spectre, a tall tower riddled with little windows. And the intentions of it? The back of my brain tells me it's meaningless, the front that it signifies humanity and its spiritual dilemmas. I think I should ignore it, drift on.

I hear shouting . . . 'Drift! What do you mean?' I succumb immediately. What do I mean? The shout is the mind being sensible, pouring logic through every nook and cranny. The mind's a noisy thing, a huge moth-eaten bag full of words.

Ah, I must pause. Angelika's just arrived with the pork. Thank you, Angelika, thank you for remembering that a man of God must eat. What lovely hair. What a beautiful silk ribbon.

Your fingers split your aura in such a gentle and rewarding fashion. You're accompanied by angels obviously. If I look closer I perceive the gilded feathers, the covering God gave them. Thank you for the smile. Thank you for leaving so quietly.

And now, out of this window, what's that, what do I see? Old Frau Braun passing water. It's life. I accept it. What a sweet unknowing smile. Always in the same place at the same time of day. That bush isn't big enough. She's a wholehearted soul.

So then, ten minutes for the pork, then back to my investigations. Eating's such a chore, but it has to be done. I'm tired of pork. Does the pig have a soul? What a plebian life he leads – and what a fate. He has a certain jauntiness, a cheery aspect. All are God's creatures.

To return to that vexed subject called logic. Am I to understand it's a gift from the creator, or is it the light of heaven trapped, as it were, in a dark flask? I prefer the latter explanation. I can make no sense of the former. The world expands in the soul, not in the erection of constructions that defy the perpendicular. I have regular discussions with Hacker-schmidt, the architect, try to find some meaning in his megalomaniacal schemes. He resists all suggestions to better himself spiritually. He thinks I'm a wordy fool.

It's almost dusk. I must light a candle. Thank the Lord I have some. Richter forbade them, thought it would stop my nightly scribbling. Foolish pastor, foolish voice of dimwitted bureau-crats. I believe, through the grace of God, that I'm a light in this community, a human voice for an angel. 'Stick to your shoemaking,' he said. And why? Are priests the only ones permitted to hear a voice from paradise? Is our creator so selective? I'll admit my writing lacks a learned style, that clarity occasionally eludes me, but so what? I'm human. The voice of my angel sometimes varies in pitch. It's hard to hear.

I'm tired now. I must work tomorrow. I've travelled so far in the imagination today. Oh blessed imagination, sacred tool against the stagnant calm of reason – our most precious gift. As I think, I hear the shrieks of the living dead, see flesh wrinkle, dissolve. As I dream, I see a golden portcullis, screeching, squealing bats circling an azure dome. And this, I say to myself, is what I must endure for a while. Morning will come – with God's grace.

Bah, what's that? Some fool's knocking at the door. Have they seen my candle? Should I snuff it out? This town is too small, Richter's agents are everywhere. I must be quick – hide my papers. Oh God, they're banging hard enough to break the door down. Hold back I say, let a poor shoemaker sleep. Am I to be hounded forever? I've been betrayed; by Angelika perhaps?

The Artist and the Holy Woman

TEETH

Sister Teresa is dying, a group of nuns are gathered round her bed. Very old, but still quite alert, she talks softly to her companions:

Teresa   I'm prepared, good and ready to meet my maker. My whole life has been a preparation for this moment. Have you written to my sister?

Eileen   (*a novice*) Yes sister, she's arranging for the little parcel to be sent immediately. She says she had a lot of trouble finding them.

Teresa   (*surprised*) Really!

Eileen   Yes, did you hide them or something? She mentioned finding them under a brick in the coal-cellar; very strange.

Teresa   (*obviously lying*) No, no, no. You know me . . . I'm just a bit eccentric. I was down in the cellar looking for a packet of firelighters. I must have taken them out to avoid the dust.

Mary   (*another novice*) What dust?

Teresa   (*quickly*) The coal dust of course. You have to be careful, it can clog them up.

Mary   (*disbelieving*) Oh, I see. To change the subject: Are you looking forward to the great beyond?

Teresa	Most definitely. I think I've done a good job down here, always tried to do my little bit. I've had my ups and downs though. Do you remember that business with Father Rafferty's shirts? I tried and tried but I could never get them clean enough for him. He was awkward.
Mother Bernadette	(*an elderly nun*) I do sister – I do. What a fuss he made. I think the Bishop sent him to Malaya in the end . . . or was it Botswana? Small chap wasn't he – big bum!
Mary	(*shocked*) Oh Mother, how could you? Sister Teresa's only minutes from the great moment and here you are blaspheming.
Bernadette	(*laughing*) Oh, don't take life so seriously. I quite liked his bum but I couldn't stand the stench of his socks.
Teresa	(*fading away*) Yes, yes, the socks were terrible. I told him to get some foot powder but he wouldn't listen. Some men are so stubborn. (*suddenly*) oh, oh, oh . . .
Eileen	(*loudly*) I think she's going! (*praying*) Holy Mary Mother of God protect her soul on the great journey. (*stops, turns to Bernadette*) She's smiling. Isn't she beautiful?
Bernadette	Yes, the angels must be calling her name. (*suddenly*) Oh, by the way, when will the parcel be arriving – she'd said it was most important.
Eileen	Tomorrow I think. Funny idea though. Still, I suppose she wants to look her best.
Mary	Yes, that must be it. Mind you . . . I wonder if they really wear false teeth in heaven?

TROUSERS

This is a conversation concerning trousers. It takes place in the office of a large clothing manufacturer. It's important to remember there's a change in the trouser trade; fashion moves on. Adolfo, the layabout son of the boss, is lecturing his father on the new styles, berating him for still producing flared trousers.

Adolfo   You're a fool to yourself Dad. Why do you continue with the flares? The kids want loose things. I wouldn't be seen dead in what you're producing. Why, if I went to Umberto's in your gear they'd laugh me off the dance floor.

Dad   (*dressed in a cream suit with flared trousers; in a wig and approaching seventy, he makes a startling contrast to his leather clad son. Replies, angry*)
Mario, Mario! What do you know about fashion? I've been in the trade a long time and all that we're witnessing is a lull in the market. Flared trousers are immortal. Back in dear old Napoli they can't get enough of them. Who cares about London, these foolish young designers who try to change the world? I know (and love) my trousers.

Groove

Adolfo	(*laughing*) I'm sure you do, let's face it you've been wearing the same suit for the last ten years. Why don't you open your mind, move with the times? I don't give a toss about Napoli, uncle Nino and all those backward cousins of mine. This is Clerkenwell, London – we're at the centre of everything here!
Dad	(*sharply*) Don't mock your forebears. You should be proud of your heritage. As Benito once said, 'Italy, Italy, mine cradle – mine grave.'
Adolfo	What a load of rubbish! What did that fat slob ever do for anybody?
Dad	(*quickly*) He once helped your grandmother with her washing.
Adolfo	When?
Dad	It was in the nineteen twenties, near Pisa. It was the time when your grandfather ran a small laundry.
Adolfo	Well, well. I never knew that.
Dad	Oh yes, it was very successful. It was the financial basis for his trouser empire, the beginning.
Adolfo	(*scornful*) Fascinating stuff. Now, back to flares: What about a change? I want to be proud of our trousers. I don't want to be known as the son of the man owning the last flared trouser factory in Europe. Who buys the horrible things anyway?
Dad	I sell mainly to the underdeveloped countries: places like Chad, Zanzibar, Cuba – France.
Adolfo	France! That's not underdeveloped.
Dad	I know son but they love their flares. They're

78

	very popular with waiters and gigolos. I shipped two thousand pairs to Lille only last week.
Adolfo	I'm impressed, and depressed. I can't believe that half the civilized world is still wearing flares. Maybe I've been blind, maybe London's not the fashion centre it's cracked up to be? Perhaps I should take to flares again, start a counter-revolution. Are there any rejects lying about, any samples? I think I'll try a pair on.
Dad	No, not here, but you can borrow mine if you like – just to see how they look.
Adolfo	No Dad, I couldn't. You're very kind but really, your underpants! I don't think I could stand the sight.
Dad	(*angry again*) What, my latino jockey briefs! They're the perfect undergarment for the modern man, better than those bits of rag you wear! I can't believe it. What's wrong with your taste, your sense of style?
Adolfo	Oh, it's useless. Have you ever looked at them? They look like somebody's taken my grandmother's bathroom curtains, cut them into pieces and made them into knickers. The design! Seaweed and dolphins, mermaids and coca-cola bottles. They're a joke.
Dad	They're attractive and functional, nothing to do with curtains at all. Your mother likes them.
Adolfo	How do you know? Have you ever asked her? Your underpants are for little boys.
Dad	Well, that's O.K. I am her little boy – in a way. She calls me her teddy.

Adolfo	Good God! You're like a couple of babies.
Dad	Well, never mind. Why worry? The trouser trade's in good shape. Are you going to Umberto's tonight? I might join you. I think I'll bring your mother along, she hasn't had a night out in months. What's the new dance these days? Twist? Frug? Hully-Gully? Mashed Banana? I can do the lot. Yes, it's time I had a bit of fun. Are you coming back home with me? You can borrow a pair of my flares – I've got some lovely new pinky ones.

No more talk. The father springs from his desk and skips across to his son clicking his fingers to some long-forgotten rhythm. The son buries his head in his hands, hands that mask tears of frustration.

Will the generations ever harmonize?

Are the old and young destined to forever be at loggerheads with each other?

Part 2: Ironies

INCIDENTS FROM AN
ENDLESS DREAM

PRAYER

Send me my death mask wrapped in wet sheets; fresh from the deep blue sea, fresh from the dream forests. Take me across the childhood playgrounds, past solitary children – angry, starved faces. Show me the houses where the Irish live. Show me the places where they eat like dirty animals. Show me prejudice and pomp and ludicrous plans for a future.

I live with memories: some good, some bad. I avoid the teeth in the mouth of the devil. I cover myself with guilt and prayer. I utter racist threats (borrowed from the talk of my betters) to the cruel shapes that cover the walls. I count stones. I count parked cars. I count the wooden posts at the front of the house.

The psychologist has inquisitive eyes, offers me a list of questions. I answer 'no' to everything. I watch pigeons trap themselves in the forecourt below. My beloved shakes with sadness, tiredness, a yearning to be free of my burden. I offer no rest.

I'm Jesus Christ come to save the universe, come to take the blackness from the eye-centre of witches. I know who the strawberry girls are. I know where they meet. I know they want to poison me.

My beloved calls a doctor who asks me about security, and alcohol, and the state of my career. My mind blows a whistle, sends out regiments of stormtroopers, little black beetle men with knives.

'And when will you rest,' she asks.

'When I've completed my work,' I answer.

Bells toll; men wait with a wooden construction, smile. I

resist the memory of a thousand hangovers. I obliterate the consequences with religion. I sip an orange juice in a ghost-filled bar, and wait for the arrival of a fine mind: I seek out brains rather than bodies. My sensuality buries itself under a death dogma. I resist all treatment. Friends touch my drooping arms, call me self-centred, unaware. Are they really friends.

Some days, the memory parades its wares. I gaze with sentimental eyes on past events, avoiding the darker edge – avoiding the spoiling fact of drink. I'm seeking out a purity (without realizing it) – looking for a balance. Are the voices in my head the clattering echo of broken cells, or are they the reflection of an unknown sea, a landscape of unworldly dead people? I seek relief in the laughter of children; amuse myself with their sense of fun.

I'm in a room surrounded by big women; I'm small and aware and totally in control. I want to touch their soft bodies – smell their skin. Who can stop me? Who wants to stop me? I'm too young to reach a Freudian conclusion – too old to turn back.

Pornography is in the distance, howling stereotypes no longer writhe before my unwilling eyes. Beautiful memories must turn into a beautiful now: there is no choice. Send me my life mask wrapped in warm sheets; fresh from the deep blue sea, fresh from the dream forests. Take me across the childhood play-grounds, past solitary children – angry, starved faces. Show me the place where they live like divines, show me hope and happiness and magnificent plans for the future.

LONDON AT NIGHT

The collective roar hurts the ears. I sit somewhere close to the edge of the platform. I speak with a drunkard's tongue, funny teeth and wild looks.

I face the cool eyes of the barman, an insolent grin on my face – fat and angry. It's my turn to save the cosmos, my turn to wave the club. All around, suburban eyes; bodies with homes to go to.

Where is truth? Where is loyalty? Where is brotherly love? The city is too big; there are too many minds at work. I seek security, invisibility, spirituality, peace. My body is a turnip; uncared for, it laughs at its own image, snarls at its ugliness, changes its shape at will. Shopgirls laugh. Street musicians hit wrong notes. A bald-headed man takes out his teeth.

Where am I? Somewhere in the city, staring at naked women, avoiding the hate and disgust in their eyes. I pay for flesh. I want to pay with my life. The cold voice of some long dead priest swamps the lust, turns it into thick brown sausages: I'll shit till I disappear.

'Tell us a joke, Fatso!' I'm the serious artist under attack – the victim of the eternal philistine. See the big men with rabbit teeth, hear the crap they talk. See the deadly toad – the bursting beached whale. Everybody's here! Everybody, and nobody to talk to. Some weekend – some silly poetry reading in the city. I arrive pissed. One glance at the assembled gathering is enough. Endless half-baked statements about love and life. The British being serious. Who cares about their simpering rural obser-vations – their mock concern for the countryside? They're self-interested, human, greedy: what's in it for them?

Mad Bastards

'Don't be bitter,' she says – 'Make the most of life.' I'm talking to a friend, watching her face for signs of madness. We're all in it together; victims and the victors. What can I say? What's she talking about? Maybe she's right. Does it matter in this awful place?

DAY

Did I see your face? Was it your face? Did you smile at me through the French windows? Sitting in my usual café, counting the small change. It's raining outside and the streets shine. I'm talking to the local mystic, sharing a vague spiritual feeling over eggs and toast. He's stoned – pompous – aware and unaware. It's morning, and I'm recovering from a bad hangover. 'More tea,' he says, observing my pile of pennies. How can I refuse? I'm composing unworkable symphonies in the local bar. Clapham is a village within a city – close to Brixton, it's an insecure place. The newspapers tell lurid tales of racist violence, muggings, burglary. The local fascists use the situation, pouring hate into every exploitable situation. It makes me nervous. I want to escape. I've no family. I hide behind dirty blinds. The bed stinks – the washing machine seems unworkable – food is hard to swallow. I use the telephone frequently; it's my only contact with friends. Flashes of egotism keep my spirit alive. I have no real routine (other than my daily trips to the bar). Serious work is a burden.

DREAMS

Maybe she'll arrive in a silver coach, shower money and security on to my humble person. Maybe she'll have sixteen lovers and choose me as her favourite. Maybe she'll spit in my eye.

I imagine her as an Amazon, legs like tree trunks and a balloon for a head. Some days, she's a dwarf – cackling and biting. Tell me, where do I look for love? The problem is picking the right dancer in the ballroom, making sure the brain fits.

I ask women friends to bring their golden bubble cars, smear some magic pomade on my head. My brain needs a rest. I need a lover to kiss me romantically, blow my tutored masculinity away. I can't be one of those bully boys, those bollock bearing apes who haunt my days. Women be kind to me.

I'm in the land of wonderful hats. The assistant is mad, talks of caterpillars and nostrils. At the rear of the shop sits the great inventor. The great inventor invents exotic puddings; jellies and pies. His is an old face. He's married to a Geisha girl from North London. 'Stroke my ear lobes,' he says, 'fondle the best part of me.' The shop is hard to find; even harder to enter. 'Goodbye,' whispers the assistant – 'leave your trousers by the door.'

I have fond memories of King Farouk, of Egypt, of a harem in Bayswater, London. Marion was the hostess. She had an obsession with the Middle East, Abdullah cigarettes, and Egypt's last reigning monarch. 'He's my dreamboat,' she would say, as she undid the zip on my flies. I liked her kitchen, it reminded me of my mother. 'Shall I dress oriental,' I said. 'No,' she replied, 'It would spoil your grubby appearance.' They were great days (it was the terrible winter of 1947). Our lust kept the cold out.

I remember P.C. Poglehurst and the Loganberry people; the blessed Walter Tilbury. I remember hours of nonsense spent in gargantuan fields. They were wonderful days. Do you know, I almost forgot Walter Winterbottom. Who was he? We made jokes about everything and everybody, spiced our youth with arrogance. Golden silly days. The memory lingers on.

My dreams live in encyclopedias alongside pictures of pygmies, old aeroplanes, giant vegetables. I live in a baby world of breasts and pisspots, sweet smiling women. I prepare for old age by staring into mirrors. 'Walter Winterbottom used to be manager of the England football team,' says a voice from the lavatory (it's my father come back from the dead). Who can argue with God?

THE END

'Bedpan, nurse!' The familiar cry of the aged. My mind flashes back to my hospital work; the fear and the misery. I see gasping toothless mouths, fat pensioners in wheelchairs; the degradation and joylessness of the public wards. There was some humour, however: old age and death completes the cycle from childhood to childhood. The sight of grandmothers chattering to toy dolls can be both moving, and amusing. 'Naughty boy,' shouts some seventy-five year old as she smacks a plastic bottom.

My father's was a happy funeral; no family bickering, everyone well behaved. I sat in the back of the limousine, tearful but unable to cry. I thought of his jokes about old age. I thought

of his fierce loyalty to my mother. I thought of my selfishness. I was confused by his death; angry at his sudden departure. I loved him, and he was gone. The snow fell heavily that day, covered his coffin in white.

I see a small room, lots of chairs, old heads with wise eyes. I hear conversations, voices talking nonsense. 'Twenty-five pence for three oranges,' says one voice. 'I missed confession,' says another. I'm in bed, a big bed, and the coverlet is deep, rich red. It's an expensive room, part of a very large house. I'm very old, and very loved. More voices: 'Are you coming?' they ask. My head reels with gentle memories; parks and gardens, small yellow flowers. I start to cry – a river bursts its banks.

Some days I think of this, the so-called space age: I have to laugh. All I can imagine is men dressed as dustbins, women in sheets of silver foil. Then, I think of the nuclear deterrent, and all I see is a field of mushrooms, boy scouts camping, girl guides singing songs. Is this the end? Is this the way to see it? We're all influenced by balding politicians, prematurely aged, wearing sagging underpants. Let's seek our own conclusion, let their fantasies rot in suburbia.

'But brotherly love is everything,' calls a child from a tenement, his face full of sunbeams: 'You're so lucky to be alive.' I look up, smile; his voice drags the truth from my self-centred brain. As I watch, his little sister joins him at the window; small and frail, she looks deep into my surprised eyes. 'It's all right,' she shouts, 'our house has no bathroom, so we wash in the sea.' So much for my angst. The sea is a thousand miles from here.

THE ISLAND

Imagine a castle made from white stone; a green hill and rose bushes; a dark sky, forbidding, nordic.

A girl dressed in pink runs towards a river, slender white arms waving, scything through the gloom. 'Save me from the terrible beast,' she cries. No one answers. We are on an island without people – in a place without sun.

This is a nightmare: My head rocks – my teeth scrape together. Am I a beast? I wake, touch my sweetheart's closed eyes, hold her hand.

My island is the home of perfection; a paradise without light. My island is in my head; a living bed of snakes. A scream can turn smoke into fire. A tear can cause a monsoon.

The world is made of islands, isolated pain. White boats encircle the land – doctors with syringes prepare to disembark. I stand at my little corner. Infused with terror I masturbate to the sound of sirens. Soon, the castle is turned into an emergency hospital – doctors prepare to operate.

FAMILY

'Oh for the joy of a good fart,' said Miriam, as she packed her suitcase. 'Yes,' whispered Bernice, 'it's all such relief when it happens.' The two sisters were preparing for their summer holidays – discussing personal habits. Miriam was ten, small, and beautiful. Bernice was eleven, plain, and wore glasses. The pleasure of farting was a favourite topic, one frowned on by their parents.

The journey to the sea was a long one, and the two girls sat patiently in the back of the family car. Their father and mother hardly spoke. 'Look at the fat dog,' said Miriam, pointing to an overfed mongrel. 'Quiet,' growled their father.

They stayed in a small hotel, very close to the beach. Bernice and Miriam slept in a dull green room and, because the weather was bad, played monopoly and draughts. Their parents argued a lot, mainly about money. It was a typical family holiday, more of an ordeal than a genuine rest; a part of the yearly routine. 'I'm in love with a policeman – I like his round legs,' confessed Bernice. 'What a strange choice,' said Miriam. 'Party tonight,' said their father, 'better make our last night a good one.'

It was a strange evening, sad and rather pointless. The girls' parents got drunk and talked about sex. Miriam kissed a boy with glasses. Bernice was jealous: 'I saw him first,' she said. 'Hard luck,' came the reply. It was silly to argue on the last day of the holiday, but they did. 'Shut up,' said their father in the car going home. Their mother said nothing; she was busy taking stock of her situation, planning to leave her husband on a 'trial basis'.

DESTINATIONS

'Where to next?' calls the bearded man, sucking at the empty beer bottle. 'Where the fuck is heaven?' The London commuters avoid his anger, avoid his questioning eyes. London: the seat of a dead empire. London: grey and ghostly and hard. I wake in the early hours, my head ringing. Self-help is the order of the day; crushing, antisocial, selfishness. Enlightened education is frowned upon – our leaders must disguise their lack of a solution.

'They're ready for another Hitler,' says the Guru Michael, his face a passive mask, his eyes glossed by dope. 'It's all in Nostradamus.' The small assembly nods agreement. 'Who left their washing on the radiator?' says a voice: nobody answers. Guru Michael coughs uncomfortably; picks at his saffron robe, blushes at the thoughts of his filthy underwear. 'Was it you, Michael?' shouts someone boldly: 'No,' he answers, 'I always take mine to the launderette.'

In the next street, Mark waits impatiently for his committee, grubby little fingers leafing through the text of his first major speech. 'I'll show them,' he says – 'I'll show them what loyalty to king and country really means.' The scene is Mark's parents' living-room; the walls covered with fascist flags, it's the headquarters of a local Empire Revival meeting. The session starts late. The discussion centres around the projected burning of an Asian newsagent's. 'When are we going to do it?' asks an obnoxious bald pinhead in a football sweater. 'Soon,' comes the answer, 'when Big Fred gives the word.' Mark smiles; he has a strong committee – his father will be pleased.

Some days, I wake from an artist's dream, huddle in bookish contentment under a comfortable blanket. I'm resting – I'm obliterating the universal scream. 'When are you going to help?' asks my child, holding up a difficult puzzle for my inspection. I start to cry; tears of love – tears of impotent frightened rage.

INTERLUDE

The big house has a swimming pool; maybe a little lake. Three friends are sitting at the kitchen table – a discussion is taking place.

Walter   It's the Chinese, they're the ones to watch.

Maureen   Nonsense, they're too small.

Gabriel   I don't agree, they're getting bigger every year: I read about it.

Walter   Correct. It's been foretold. The yellow men shall rise from the east bringing war and pestilence – a high cost of living – a sense of death. Cars and motor cycles will increase in price. Washing machines will become antiques.

Maureen   Why?

Walter   Because, being socialists, they'll want to communalize the family wash – it will all be done in great bathtubs.

Gabriel   Sounds logical.

Maureen   Sounds hysterical; just imagine your truss swimming around in a sea of overalls – very funny.

Gabriel   I don't wear one now.

Maureen   You used to . . .

Walter   (*accusingly*) Yes you did!

Gabriel   But I don't now. Everything's in order in that department.

Maureen	Can we see?
Gabriel	Certainly!

At that, Gabriel commences a slow striptease. Both Maureen and Walter start to yawn. Finally, Maureen speaks:

Maureen	Put your clothes back on, we've seen it all before.
Gabriel	Yes, and you don't like it.
Walter	Correct.
Maureen	No arguments, boys. Let's get back to China: What's going to happen to our eating habits? Will it be sweet and sour pork forever?

Both Gabriel and Walter get up and leave. Maureen remains sitting, a look of mad desperation on her face.

ANSWERS

I'm watching a blank living-room wall, watching for omens; signs of future happiness. I'm looking back on a broken marriage, alcoholism; a nervous breakdown. I'm living in Germany in a kind of Joycean exile. I'm resisting nostalgia – biting my lip in the process.

I hear the crash of rock 'n' roll bands, the brash music of my youth. I see myself on a stage – hear my detractors and admirers. 'Give us a tune,' they say. 'Make us dance.' How can I resist? My veteran's pride makes me a show off – makes me a professional – makes me sad. Is it all a search for adoration? Must I always bury my deepest yearning in the midst of a cheering, jeering crowd?

Depression; dark and repetitive, it cuts into the days like a knife. It has no respect for past joys, no respect for fine memories: it obliterates everything. A short walk has no effect, it only serves to emphasize the happiness of others. A loving hand feels wooden, stiff; everything's a problem. 'Come on old monkey face' – a voice on the end of the telephone smashes me into reality. 'Remember me?' I don't, but I talk; glad of anyone to relieve the emptiness. Any sound is better than no sound at all. 'Who are you?' I ask. 'What do you want?' The telephone goes dead; an answer never arrives.

I'm standing on the top of a hill, cooling rain peppers my hot face. Below me is a rich green valley; flowers and little streams. A girl stands beside me, big and young with long loving arms. 'That's the future,' she says. I have an urge to fall backwards into the mud – a terrible need to scream. I don't. I can't. Her smile defeats my anxiety.

EDUCATION

'We're going to talk about racial prejudice and its influence on the native population of the South Pacific,' said Professor Longbottom. 'Oh not again,' snorted Brian, gazing wearily in the direction of the lecturer. It was Monday morning at Snelgrove university, and the students were bored. The gathering of fresh knowledge was far from their mind; the weekend and the summer recess was all they could think about.

Amanda met Brian in the main hall afterwards: 'Wasn't it a drag, Bri,' she exclaimed, gazing over his shoulder at Melvyn Tompkins. 'Yes,' he replied, 'trust old egghead Longbottom to bore the arse of us on the last week of term.' Amanda left Brian

97

Waiting for Heaven

and moved across to Melvyn. 'Could I borrow your hacksaw tomorrow,' she said. Brian was taken aback: why hadn't she asked him?

Life at the university was often interesting, but the brutal murder of Brian Brownsword caused an excitement unheard of before. His body was found in the bushes by Professor Longbottom, the head sawn off and placed in a dustbin nearby. It was a Wednesday morning, two days after the tedious lecture on the South Pacific. 'Always was a cheeky beggar,' muttered Longbottom as he lifted the head from the bin, 'never paid attention.'

Although he protested his innocence Melvyn Tompkins was the prime suspect. It was revealed he was having a passionate love affair with Amanda Moon – sometime girlfried of Brian – and deeply resented sharing her attentions. His solution was to destroy the opposition, hence Brownsword's murder.

'I liked them both,' said Amanda afterwards, 'if only I'd remembered to borrow Melvyn's hacksaw then perhaps all of this would never have happened.' Investigating Inspector Ronald Dogger shook his head, 'You're a pretty girl, Miss Moon, some of you students don't know you're born. Why, after this, I'm glad my boy joined the army.'

'Sad business,' commented Professor Longbottom as he read his morning paper. 'I see they've committed young Tompkins to Broadmoor.' 'Best place for him,' said Mavis, his wife and confidante of thirty-five years: 'It's all this group sex – I blame it on the Swedes.'

HEAVEN

Tibet, Sunday morning: A monk is eating his breakfast; two British guests are holding him in conversation. It's 1937.

Sybil   How do you cook your cabbage here? Do you boil it; steam it — what?

Monk   Your British tea is of excellent quality. By the way, who was Earl Grey?

Sybil   (*frustrated*) What about your prayer wheels? Do they move in a clockwise or anticlockwise direction? How many prayers before you're officially on the road to heaven

Robin   Don't bother his holiness, my dear, can't you see he's eating?

Monk   (*grumpily*) Yes, I am.

Sybil   Well, I want to know: we haven't come all this way for nothing. I have to report to the Ladies Guild when I get back.

Robin   Yes, and Mrs Plum will be annoyed if you don't deliver your little speech – I know.

Sybil   Precisely! She's a horror. Do you know, she told Mrs Sidebottom we ate tinned mangoes for breakfast: as if we would! She's always trying to make us into artists or bohemians or something. Have you seen her husband's leg?

Robin   No dear . . .

Monk   I have.

Sybil	Really! How could you have? – He's thousands of miles from here.
Monk	(*quietly*) It is healed.
Sybil	I don't believe you, Doctor Crump said that that kind of injury . . .
Monk	(*firmly*) It is healed.
Robin	Better take his word for it, dear – he knows about these things.
Sybil	Rubbish! Medical facts are medical facts. Give me good old Church of England any day, there's none of this miracle nonsense. I'm off – Lhasa next: that's the capital you know.
Robin	How far is it, your highness?
Monk	As far as the flight of bat – as near to heaven as the eyes of a golden Llama.
Sybil	That's no good: give us proper directions!
Robin	Where's the map?

Poland, New Years Eve: Stefan and his wife are talking about their children, contemplating a dreary 1985. It's very cold – church bells can be heard in the distance.

Stefan	The holy Father has predicted a year of toil and struggle, a time for prayer and meditation on the future: Where do we stand in all of this? What about little Stanislaus? Is he praying? Is he truly aware of his mortal soul?
Wife	I wouldn't like to say; last time I saw him he was drinking with some workers from the shipyard – he's twenty-eight now.
Stefan	But his soul! What about his soul!
Wife	You'd better ask him, he'll maybe visit us in spring. Do you want some carrots? (*she goes to a large pot on the stove and stirs the contents quickly*)

Stefan	(*continuing*) Carrots – always carrots: I need onions – something to make my breath stink!
Wife	It does already.
Stefan	(*angry*) What!
Wife	It does! Little Anna complained the other day, she said, 'Why does my grandfather have such a stinky mouth, it smells like my pet rabbit's bottom.' You see, children notice these things.
Stefan	Oh God in holy heaven, what am I to do? Does this mean that it stinks when I take communion, when I take the sacred host into my mouth?
Wife	Certainly.
Stefan	I'm damned – I'm doomed. To take the blessed host is to kiss the virgin Mary on her virginal mouth. Oh forgive me, Holy Mother!
Wife	What about me? You never apologize after we've had a session – I smell it too.
Stefan	Oh, that's different, (*whispers*) you're not a virgin.
Wife	Bullshit! All this stuff and nonsense about virgins. What about yourself – you're not one either! Hypocrite – fart breath – turd mouth. I'm leaving, go and kiss your arse – you're neck's long enough!
Stefan	What about solidarity – what about the workers' meeting tomorrow?
Wife	Forget about it – let's have some honesty first: Virgin indeed!

MADNESS

No laughter; just steady, grinding obsession. Leaves fall from autumn trees; mashed underfoot they look like dark porridge – dead, wet, blood. Cats appear; with heads like lions, they frighten the pigeons away. Electric cables hang invitingly – frogs speak from muddy pools. I'm in the garden of Eden eating the first apple: I'm part of the start of life.

There's so much twaddle written about madness – so much Laingian vagueness. Of course it can be argued that a little madness is 'Good for the art' but, to one who has really exprienced it, it's a part of existence that's best left alone. As I write about it, each painful memory brings back a flood of confusion and fear. How did I survive? How did my loved ones survive? I'm still trying to reconstruct a shattered existence, still struggling hard.

Last night I looked through a gauze sheet at the past, watched mummified figures dancing to a single drumbeat. A naked black boy danced on a long table as white grasping hands reached out to touch. It was hell; dark and shabby and frightening. Soon it would be my turn to perform – rifles and spears would prod me into action . . . where and how would it end?

SURVIVAL

'Bright and early – that's the way,' said matron, as she dragged the sheets off the bed. It was my first term at St Cuthberts, a cheap boarding school in the south of England – and I was scared. Bigsby had threatenend to give me a good whacking if I didn't share my biscuits during the second break, so matron had dragged me rather too suddenly into reality. 'Leave off,' I cried, rubbing my eyes, 'can't you let a fellow rest?' 'No,' came the reply: 'The breakfast's getting cold.'

The second break arrived after a dreadful English lesson: lots of grammar – lots of noun clauses. The teacher – Mr Harbottle – had an irritating habit of spitting while he spoke, and I was in the front row. Anyway, at the break I tried to hide behind one of the pillars that surrounded the biology lab. It was useless, Bigsby spotted me and ran to my side. 'So, little sprat,' he shouted, 'trying to avoid me, eh?' With that, he cuffed me round the left ear. 'Biscuits,' he demanded, 'quick!' I had no choice – I handed them over. You see, he was the biggest boy in the form, and by far the strongest.

'It's survival of the fittest,' said the padre, pouring out the tea and offering me a cream scone, 'with God's help, we pull through.' The scene was the padre's office; painted in dark browns and greens it resembled a cosy prison cell. Some help you are, I thought. I come to you for protection and guidance, and what do I get? – a lecture on the beastliness of mankind! I left his office in a turmoil, resigned to running away.

My mother was angry, 'What a waste of your father's money!' she shouted, tickling the poodle's ears and stamping her tiny feet. 'What are we going to do now?' It was terrible, I'd hitchhiked nearly two hundred miles for this! I retired to bed in disgust.

That night I had a wonderful dream: I was James Dean, cool and handsome – admired by the girls. Sandra Dee was my secret lover and, although the film company forbade our relationship, we met every Sunday at a quiet beach on the Californian coast; me disguised as Harpo Marx – she as Shirley Temple. It was magnificent; the world and its wonders lay before us – there was nothing we couldn't do.

The next morning my father gave me a stiff lecture; tight-lipped and calm, he seemed remarkably in control (normally, he would have boxed my ears and sent me back). 'Don't do it again,' he concluded, 'otherwise I'll have to stop your pocket money.' That evening I heard war had been declared with Russia, and that my father had been called up. I was allowed to stay at home and look after my mother. I never returned to St Cuthberts again.

CONNECTIONS

There are minutes, moments and memories. The body twitches, itches, fails. There are contradictions, conclusions, betrayals. Life lingers, leaps, explodes. We think we know, but experience proves us wrong. Each second contains the sharp bite of death. Salvation is hard to imagine. Priests and politicians espouse great plans for the future, tells us heaven is just round the corner. Honest pessimism is frowned upon, considered anti-happiness – contrary to the real meaning of existence. We are trapped. We seek connections, consult astrological books for

guidance. We try to defeat human nature, turn its darker side into positive – invent kharma to justify life's evils. I understand everything – I understand nothing. Are we making unnecessary fuss out of the accident of birth?

MEDIA

'Imagine you're a bottle of washing-up liquid,' said Harold Molesworth, director of Molesworth Marketing. 'How would you feel?' 'Strange,' came the answer from the back of the office, 'very strange.' There was a long silence and then the inevitable explosion. 'Who said that?' demanded Molesworth – 'I won't have my pep-talks disturbed in this way.' There was a further silence: no one answered. Molesworth shook his head. 'Very sad,' he whispered. 'One thing required here is honesty. Whatever happened to the youth of today?'

Gerald was tired of designing beer mats, sick of labels for sauce and sardines. 'I want to paint,' he said to Fiona. 'I want to really express myself.' Fiona was baffled, she'd just joined Molesworth Marketing and thought it was a pretty good job. 'Why?' she asked, 'don't you like it here?' Gerald didn't bother to answer; if she couldn't see the pain and yearning in his eyes – what was the point?

'Your paintings are too small, the Americans buy them by the square foot.' Gerald was shocked; he'd left Molesworth Marketing only to be confronted by the same hard commercial selling style he'd grown to hate in advertising. 'But what about the quality?' he asked. 'You're very talented,' the dealer answered.

The months went by and Gerald continued to visit the

dealers. He always seemed to be behind (or ahead) of the trends: he failed to sell anything. Fiona visited him one day: 'How's it going?' she asked, gazing with distaste at the mess of paints, paper and canvas. 'Awful,' said Gerald, 'I think I'll ask for my old job back.'

'Welcome back to Molesworth's,' said Harold – smiling. 'It's good you've seen the error of your ways and decided to pursue a real career again.' Gerald remained silent. 'Now,' Harold continued, 'I want you to imagine you're a potato in a family-sized pack – how would you feel?'

MEMORIES

As the years go by, memories play an increasingly prominent part in my thinking: the past dominates the moment. I think, and then I stop to think again. Age brings familiarity with life's situations – it narrows the breadth of experience. I know but I have no answers. I'm confused but thinking about it increases the confusion. I look for connections; patterns, but they change so constantly – all I see is a repetition of change.

Good memories give strength to the present – reaffirm the need to live. The absence of solid proof of an after-life makes memories essential. Memories can cause and prevent suicide.

PHOTOGRAPHS

When sad self-absorption takes the upper hand I gently force my mind into a half-working dream, into silent images of the past. I see a church on a hill, children milling around its gates, a small boy with sagging socks; I see ducks, and a canal bank, fishermen on stools. Then – almost always – an overgrown garden emerges; a brown perambulator rocks fiercely. I see a small red-brick house; the kitchen door open, a man eating. I enter the tiny room and look into his eyes; he's drunk – over friendly – sad. He pats my head, and I'm aware of making myself smile, half out of fear – half out of recognition. He's a relation – an uncle – one I don't see very often.

Everything's a mist, softly drenched in 'B' movie lighting; grey, indistinct, sometimes frighteningly black and white. A woman wearing ugly post-war spectacles stares into a cot. Her face is enormous, round like a football; false teeth squeak. Her hair's cropped and crisp and sensibly styled. It's a birthday, and time for celebration, there's chocolate and sticky red sweets – fried bacon and mushrooms for breakfast. The living-room table has a clean white tablecloth. The red-brick house again: there's a field at the back – a big posh house in the distance. Buttercups are everywhere, stinging nettles hide in the long grass. Summer: idyllic and endless. Summer: breaker of sweet promises. A girl stands by the canal bank, her skinny legs brown and tempting. Shall we walk on to the woods? Shall we touch for a while? Let's avoid the jeers of our immature friends. Shall we find out what passion is?

CONFLICT

The girl writhed naked on a circular dais, contorting her body. The peep-show was almost empty, only one man watched the show, his eyes glued to the display of flesh. It was a new experience for both individuals. This was the girl's first ever performance. She'd once worked in a bookshop, but the recession and the taunts of a drunken boyfriend had led her to this – the last resort. The man had never been in a peep-show before, shyness and an acute sense of self-degradation had prevented him from entering. Now, it was different, he was initiated and he hated it. Meat was all he could think of; a slaughterhouse and innocent screaming animals, his girlfriend and his mother – abused and defiled. The girl felt ridiculous, frightened, angry. Why had she agreed to do this? The awful pop-music was crude. She stood up, and left. 'You can't go, Lana hasn't turned up,' said the fat boss, in a clumsy mixture of German and American. 'Fuck off!' she shouted, as she dressed. 'You talk like a dog-handler and you look like a pig – fuck off!' The boss was temporarily stunned. After some seconds, he spoke, 'It's O.K.,' he drawled, 'Your tits weren't big enough anyway.'

It was freezing cold outside. The man hurried to the nearest coffee shop, tortured by feelings of insecurity and fear he had to sit and think. 'Why?' he kept asking himself, 'why?'

In the coffee shop the man was surprised to see the girl from the peep-show. He wanted to talk to her, to tell her he'd agreed with her leaving – to tell her he'd left in protest at the same time. It was useless; he wasn't brave enough.

POISON

Harold Crossley knew everything, was an expert on anything. Everyone in the Crossley household subscribed to his idiotic theories because they were afraid of him: he was master of the house. 'Man is king,' he would say, 'the living proof of God's supreme will.' He was often drunk – often violent, an intolerable burden to his wife and two children. At forty-one Harold was the stupid inheritor of a fearsome system; he believed in his megalomaniacal behaviour because no one told him it was wrong: His family were his subjects – he was the divine inheritor of the kingdom.

'I hate him – I know it's wrong, but I hate him,' said Mandy Crossley to her friend Sharon, 'I can't live with him another day.' Sharon was sympathetic, 'Why don't you poison him?' she said, 'it's been done before.' Mandy went home that night her mind full of Sharon's suggestion. Could she do it? She thought she'd try.

Harold Crossley died of food poisoning: it was all very sudden. Mandy was relieved, she'd thought of arsenic and broken glass. 'You were quick,' laughed Sharon after the inquest. 'You did a good job.' Mandy protested, 'It was a frozen chicken – it was pure luck!' Sharon smiled, her face a picture of total disbelief. 'Really?' she said, mockingly.

At the funeral, friends and relations couldn't help noticing how happy the Crossleys were. 'William's laughing,' whispered a neighbour, noticing the beam on the son's face. 'And Mandy,' said her companion. Mrs Crossley kept a straight face; long-suffering to the end. 'Harold Crossley was a good and honourable man,' boomed the priest, at the start of his sermon: nobody really believed him.

ENGLAND (AN UNREASONABLE VIEW)

The sun shines; a beach ball soars high into the light blue sky, lands gently admist a crowd of holiday-makers: 'Mind your heads,' shouts someone. I'm sitting at a distance from the group, observing the ritual of the English at play; it's amusing and horrific at the same time. They all seem so white – so fat, but then, why not? I have an ingrained suspicion of the perfect, bronzed specimen. Don't they belong in Italy somewhere?

Noble, dirty, hypocritical England; with its deformed industrial landscape and beautiful natural scenery it creates a toughness and a fragility, tortured introvert concealed under a gloss of acquired reasonableness. The English mistrust what they call 'an emotional display' – they prefer it all to boil in the brain, to simmer and (hopefully) never explode. They prefer civilized social barbarity – secrets; confusion must be kept down.

GURU

The guru sits. Friends and admirers gather round his chair; eager and attentive, they're ready to hang on his every word. We are witnessing a visitation from Walter T Horton: seer, evangelist, and advocate of 'Balancism'. The university hall is packed. A long-delayed meeting is about to take place. Wendy Wharton asks the first question:

Wendy	You are an American, do you believe in the after life?
Horton	What has my being American got to do with it?
Wendy	Sorry.

Craig Willoughby asks the next question; like Wendy Wharton he's in his early twenties. Horton is in his early seventies:

Craig	I'm a buddhist and my mother is a catholic; should there be any friction between us?
Horton	Yes, everybody argues sometimes.
Craig	But why, master?
Horton	Don't call me master; I'm just a steel-erector from Iowa – next question!

Terence Cleavage, a little annoyed at the abrupt answers, asks a question:

Terence	Why are you so rude to people? Professor Hackett said you were the champion of a new self-awareness, that you could help us lead more positive lives.
Horton	I'm not Professor Hackett.
Terence	Is that all you've got to say?
Horton	Yes.

Shirley Fowler, slightly older than the rest of the group, and one

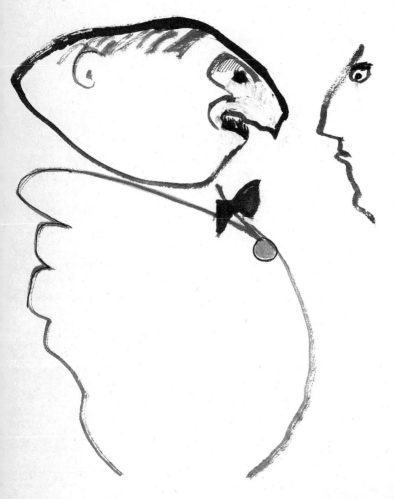

of the committee who invited Horton to speak at the university is the next to address the chair:

Shirley	Are you really Walter T Horton, creator of Balancism – the man who has given over thirty-two lecture tours of the United States?
Horton	Yes.
Shirley	Then where's the positivity – the stirring advice – the light in a dark age?
Horton	You're looking at it.
Shirley	Yes, but where's the evidence – how do we know? The information sheet from New York said you'd speak in detail about your intended conquest of the European mind; that you'd involve us all in your plans for peace. Am I to believe that we've been mislead? You've had amazing things said about you.
Horton	(*lighting a pipe*) Well, I didn't write them – you can't blame me.

Cries of 'fraud' and 'fake' are heard. 'He's useless,' shouts someone. Horton rises from his chair and prepares to leave, saying, 'You wanted Walter T Horton – you got him – and now you don't like him; what's your problem?' Shirley Fowler bursts into tears. 'You're just like my husband,' she sobs. 'Negative – pompous and boring.' Horton leaves, muttering, 'It's all to do with balance – all to do with balance.' The meeting breaks up. Craig Willoughby, frustration and anger showing on his face shouts, 'And they say he's going to Oxford next – God help those dark blues.'

MEETING

We're figures in a Fuseli painting; dancing, dreaming, leering, loving. We've got pointed ears – sharp, pointed noses. You're smiling at me across a table: long hair drips down your face – fails to hide your eyes. I recall lovelorn poems by Rossetti – a line of mad prostitutes in Vienna. We're inventing reasons to meet. I'm a bit afraid. I love you, but don't turn me into an object of embarrassed admiration: respect my need to crawl with the rest of humanity. Let's not interpret each other's every move, word, whim. Let's disguise the predictable response. You are a beloved mystery – I would wish to be the same. We must re-invent romance – with your permission.

Early days: screaming, pushing, lonely – drunk. So much abuse – so many violent acts. I was reliving my past relationship – forgetting your identity, confusing you with a nightmare. You had to be strong (and you were): I was as weak as a new-born child.

And now, nearly one year later? Well, the sun shines, making shadows on the snowy garden. We sit, talk, understand each other – observe the view with a positive vision. We meet afresh everyday.

ARTIST

Max was an artist and competitive; 'You have to be,' he said to
Hubert, one long winter afternoon. Hubert – a bricklayer by
trade – was used to Max's aggressive attitude: he understood.
'Calm down,' he soothed, noticing Max's reddening face – his
clenched fists. 'Summer's not far away.' 'Bollocks to summer,'
yelled Max, 'that won't help.'

'I'm instinctive,' said Mavis Broadstairs, running her hands
nervously through her long dark hair. Max stared into his coffee
cup, 'I'm a genius,' he snarled. Mavis and Max met regularly at
the 'El Toro', a smart café in the centre of town: it was a centre
for artistic discussion. Cups clattered – the Espresso machine
hissed: Mavis and Max sat in silence. When Hubert arrived,
Max had fallen asleep, his head thrown back, saliva dripping
from one corner of his mouth. 'Not too lively today,' commented Hubert as he sat down. 'Let's go to the lake,' said Mavis.

The little town of Bumberly was shocked at Mavis
Broadstairs' suicide. Max took it very coolly. 'It was reading
that Virginia Woolf,' he grumbled. 'Mavis should have accepted
her mediocrity, been a housewife or something!' Hubert was
shocked, the cruel burst of chauvinism nearly took his breath
away. 'Cut it out,' he protested. 'How can you be such a pig?'
Max didn't answer; instead, he sat back in his chair and thought
of his mother ironing: a happy woman.

THE DARK AGES

I'm describing a room; brown glossy furniture, heavy curtains, embossed wallpaper, pink tulips in a vase. An old women sits by a large open fire; small with white nondescript features, she epitomizes living death – a body defeated by age. Her son, wiry and fit – young for his age, has come to visit her.

Conversation begins:

Old woman	How's your job?
Son	Very good; Dora sends her love.
Old woman	Tell her I'm very pleased.
Son	Have you still got father's old watch?
Old woman	Yes, it still works.
Son	Can Hugh have it?
Old woman	No, he's not old enough.
Son	Pity, he needs it for sports day – it's got a stopwatch on it.
Old woman	Sorry.
Son	It doesn't matter.
Old woman	I'm still sentimental about Harry's old things, especially that watch. Did you know it was a parting gift from Jack Wormsley?
Son	Of Fosset and Wormsley?
Old woman	Yes.
Son	Well I'll be blowed – I didn't know they were such good friends.
Old woman	Oh yes, they often slept together.
Son	Good gracious mother – didn't you mind?

Old woman	No, I was assured there was no hanky panky going on.
Son	But in 1947! Wasn't it illegal?
Old woman	(*angry*) There was no hanky panky going on!
Son	Well mother, I wish you'd told me father was a queer; it makes one feel all funny.
Old woman	(*still angry*) He wasn't queer – or whatever you call it: he just liked sleeping with Jack Wormsley, said he liked his company!
Son	(*mocking*) Very funny.
Old woman	I won't have your father's memory tainted in this way; he was a good and honest man.
Son	And queer.
Old woman	Stop it!
Son	What am I going to tell Dora and Hugh – what will the in-laws say?
Old woman	Good God! What a feeble mind you've got – and dirty too. You and your kind live in the dark ages: why shouldn't men like each other?
Son	I'm going home. What other dark secrets do you keep in that aged brain? I thought you thought of nothing but mealtimes and dusting furniture: goodbye!
Old woman	Do you still want that green jumper mending? Did Dora get you those socks?

The son races from the room, slamming the door as he leaves. The old woman sighs; reaching for her knitting, she screams for the first time in years.

A PROBLEM

Culture's got me in a headlock; big fat easy arms hold me down. I'm afraid of it – afraid of the bourgeois connections – afraid of polite learned language. I continually return to my working-class roots, fight to embrace the nastiness – the studied lack of education: I'm afraid, I have to communicate my confusion – my unease. I'm the child of a self-conscious, cruel, class-ridden society. I have to explain why I exist. It's my problem.

FACTORY

It was a horrible place; a heartbreaking tomb. Walter, aspirant novelist and playwright, made his living there. Every day, as he stood by his lathe, he dreamed of international recognition – of great literary awards. His manuscripts were constantly returned; no one seemed to like them. 'It's those posh bastards in London,' he said to his girlfriend, 'All they do is drink cocktails and talk rubbish.' Carol had doubts; she couldn't understand what he was writing about anyway.

It was a difficult and depressing existence; Walter, frustrated by the vagaries of the literary world, often shouted at Carol. It was blathering, pointless, cruel rage: 'Get up off your arse and do some real work,' he'd yell – 'Sometimes I think you've got no brain at all!' This would usually occur when Carol was ironing or washing clothes: it made her very angry. Her thoughts turned to violence and revenge; finally, she decided to write a book.

The Goblin's Magic Boots was a great success. Carol, greatly encouraged, planned a series. 'What do you think I should call the next one?' she asked Roger, her new boyfriend. 'Oh something silly and simple,' he replied. '*The Goblin's Tea Party*, I think.'

Walter persisted, but without any luck: he changed his writing style regularly – even wrote a book of children's poems. The factory closed, and he took a job as a gardener's assistant. 'Have you read any Joyce,' he asked the foreman one fresh spring morning. 'No, but I once fucked a Beryl,' comes the insensitive reply. Walter looked down at his barrow – full of dead lupins, and thought of Carol, Roger and W B Yeats. 'Roll on cricket season,' he said, aloud.

ASBESTOS

It's a warm Monday evening in summer. The St Mark's Hall therapy group are drawing to the end of their session; four people sit in plain wooden chairs facing each other.

Dr Throstle   Are you sure that asbestos garden shed still exists – didn't you say it was pulled down years ago?

Placket   I'm not sure, but there's some surrounding our fireplace at home.

Dr Throstle   Is the surface broken – is it dangerous?

Placket   It's hard to tell – I don't touch it.

Ursula   (*exasperated*) Let's talk about something else: I was beaten at school – I had to hide in the cloakroom.

William   (*cheerily*) So was I: I think it's because I wore short trousers till I was fourteen.

Placket   (*loudly*) That's when I first came into contact with asbestos, when I first realized it was everywhere.

Dr Throstle   Please, one subject at a time. What was that about short trousers, William?

William   I hated them.

Placket   So did I – dangerous things – anything could creep up your legs.

Ursula   What about skirts?

Dr Throstle   (*gently*) So many problems – so many little irritations: shall we finish now? It's nearly nine, and my supper will be ready.

Placket   Oh, here we go again – just when it was getting helpful. I come here every week but the worry never goes away.

Dr Throstle   (*kindly*) That's life, Edward; still, it's better to talk about it to someone – better to get it out into the open.

Ursula   Yes, thank you doctor – you're a great help.

William   (*merrily*) All chums together, sharing and caring.

Placket   (*angrily*) Apart from fountain pens!

Dr Throstle   (*concluding*) Fountain pens, asbestos, short trousers, skirts: what does it all come to in the end? Life is short, and the sweeter we make it the better it is. Why, this church hall could be the start of a new brotherhood – a new sisterhood – a new tolerant community: don't you agree?

Placket	As long as the building's safe. There's no asbestos in the roof, is there?

STRESS

I can't relax; I need to, but I can't. I want to rest eight hours every night, join the happy band of regular contented sleepers. What's wrong? Gross schemes invade my head; scenes of cruelty and debauchery oppose my peace, nag at my post-catholic conscience. I fiddle with myself, twitch and shake and shudder: Stop those voices! There are times when I become Wilfred Trilby, when shadows in corners turn to flesh and blood, when a hospital and sedation seems the only answer. Should I try meditation?

Should I cultivate a spiritual discipline; take it all stoically – invent some purpose to it all? All I hear is a clamouring throng – the thud of heavy boots on concrete. I'm alone – passing time – waiting, waiting, waiting.

HISTORY

'I want to be part of history!' he shouted, 'I need to be a verified great.' 'All in good time?' said the sensible voice. 'All in good time.' Trees spoke; it was a very odd garden party. Mandy raced towards Henry, a large cream bun raised to strike. 'Watch it,' he said, as he turned, 'Mummy's watching.'

'What is there to explain?' asked Constance, feet firmly stuck in a soothing bowl of warm water. 'History always repeats itself.' The guests were gathered in the large kitchen; the party was over – it was raining outside. I sat in a corner trying to avoid the attentions of a thin girl with green hair. I didn't like all the talk about history, even though it had been my favourite subject at school. Everything that happened in life confirmed my deepest suspicions of humanity; that 99 percent of communication was vanity and hot air. History was mass self-flagellation. 'Cheer up,' said a jolly voice in my ear, completely disturbing my thoughts – annoying me with its confidence, 'arm wrestling starts in a minute.' With that, I abandoned my inner musings, returned to the scene in the kitchen.

Blissed Out:
The Raptures of Rock
Simon Reynolds

Blissed Out is a celebration of the 'underground' music of today. From hardcore to hip hop, acid rock to acid house, these cults contradict the widely-held view that 'rock is dead' and that there is nothing left for musicians to do but play pick'n'mix with thirty years of pop history. In interviewing and writing about his favourite bands, Public Enemy, Throwing Muses, Prince, My Bloody Valentine, Nick Cave and the Bad Seeds, Morrissey, or Pixies, Simon Reynolds captures the giddy exhilaration of their music.

'*Blissed Out* reveals Reynolds as a fan as much as a critic, and his intelligence, wit and passion about music is always welcome.'★★★★   *Q magazine*

'These essays show that intelligence is not something to be afraid of, and that, despite the cultural poisons spread by the New Right and their henchmen, Pop is still prophecy, not just baby-boomer nostalgia or niche marketing.'   JON SAVAGE

192 pages £8.99

**Seeing in the Dark:
A Compendium of Cinemagoing**
Ian Breakwell and Paul Hammond (eds)

'It was a former skating rink, a long narrow building with the screen in the middle, because projectors in 1916 didn't have the throw. The admission was two jamjars and one jamjar. For two you got a proper seat. For one you sat *behind* the screen to watch the silent film, using a hand mirror to read the inter-titles.'   DENIS NORDEN

'The manager was patrolling the aisles and found a pair of lady's panties on the floor by the back stalls. He picked them up and courteously enquired of the young woman sitting closest with her boyfriend if they were hers. With equal decorum she replied, "Oh no, mine are in my handbag." '   NOEL SPENCE

For a generation of cinemagoers, food was sweet popcorn, sex began in double seats and post-modernism was reels played in the wrong order. The hundred contributors to *Seeing in the Dark* illumi-nate the picture palace with a bizarre, funny collection of movie tales. Contributors include: Angus Calder, Kevin Coyne, Ivor Cutler, Janice Eidus, Nicole Ward Jouve, James Kelman, Deborah Moggach, Daniel Moyano, Tom Raworth, Carolee Schneeman, Lynne Tillman, David Toop and Haifa Zangana.

176 pages £10.99 (paper) large format/illustrated

The Rap Attack:
African Jive to New York Hip Hop
David Toop

The Rap Attack, the first book on rap, remains the definitive book on the subject. Rap first emerged in New York's Harlem and Bronx, and quickly spread to all corners of the globe. Rap artists are now a regular feature of musical and counter-cultural life in all major cities, and the influence of rap itself is to be found in all contemporary popular music. In the words of Charlie Gillett, read the *The Rap Attack* and 'discover the pioneers of the most potent new sound of the eighties.'

'The most authoritative book yet on the New York street phenomenon.'   *Record Mirror*

'A coherently written and well researched introduction to a fascinating musically-based culture.'
                                                            Next

172 pages/illustrated/£4.95

The Lonely Hearts Club
Raul Nuñez

'The singles scene of Barcelona's lonely low life. Sweet and seedy.' *Elle*

'A celebration of the wit and squalor of Barcelona's mean streets.' *City Limits*

'This tough and funny story of low life in Barcelona manages to convey the immense charm of that city without once mentioning Gaudi . . . A story of striking freshness, all the fresher for being so casually conveyed.' *The Independent*

'A sardonic view of human relations . . .'
  The Guardian

'Threatens to do for Barcelona what *No Mean City* once did for Glasgow.' *Glasgow Herald*

'A funny low life novel of Barcelona.' *The Times*

160 pages £6.95 (paper)